I0731503

COLD HARD CASH

ALSO BY DALE DEVINO

IN THE HARBOR POINT CRIME SERIES

Stick Em' Up (Ellis Boone #0)

Cold Hard Cash (Ellis Boone #1)

Pennies From Heaven (Ellis Boone #2)

Up In Smoke (Ellis Boone #3)

THE HARBOR POINT CRIME SERIES

COLD HARD CASH

ELLIS BOONE: BOOK ONE

DALE DEVINO

3VS
MEDIA

COPYRIGHT

First Published by 3VS Media in 2020.

Edited by Kim Kocher

ISBN: 978-1-952771-01-9

Copyright © 2020 by Dale DeVino

All of the characters in this book are fictitious and any resemblance to actual persons, living or dead, is coincidental.

All rights reserved.

No part of this book may be reproduced in any form or by any electronic or mechanical means, including information storage and retrieval systems, without written permission from the author, except for the use of brief quotations in a book review.

For Tara & Veronica
None of this is possible without you guys.

And for Mom
I think you'd be proud.

Harbor Point

CHAPTER ONE

"Ellis Boone? I know that name? Where do I know you from?"

Reggie, a mountain of a man, rested his gargantuan frame against a brick wall. He held my identification in his club like hand. With his head cocked to one side and his eyes squinted, he tried to pull my name from his memory banks. I stopped him.

"I'm no one. I'm just here for the tits," I said.

"So whatchu doin' down here? Slumming? Ain't no cracker clubs you can go to?" he said.

"The cracker clubs don't want me. Like I said. I'm no one."

Reggie raised an eyebrow at me like I was crazy. Given the history of this place maybe I was.

The Cheetah Club was founded half a century ago by Paps McCollum and has been the standard bearer for all things in adult entertainment since the day the doors opened. From the riots in 1977, when Old Man Paps held off a gang of looters by himself with a sawed off shotgun and several flaming liquor bottles to the untimely passing of Old Paps while in the

Champagne Room, everyone in The Bottoms knew The Cheetah Club. Even if the contents were not to your liking.

Reggie curled up his lips into a half smile, half smirk, flashing me his pearly whites.

"I don't want no problems outta you tonight you hear me whiteboy?" he said.

He didn't have to say anything else. The point was made when he lifted his shirt and revealed the matte black handle of a pistol.

"You ever use that thing?" I said and took a step toward the door where another human sized boulder was waiting to pat me down.

"Not tonight," he said while fixing his attention away from me to an intoxicated man who was urinating on the wall of the club. I didn't care to see the outcome of that mistake, so I slipped through the double glass doors and made my way to a slightly raised counter where a set of soft almond eyes met mine.

"Twenty-five," she said.

I forked over the money without even questioning the exorbitant cover charge because despite my proclivity for the naked female in all forms, I was here to do a job.

I was looking for a guy.

Climbing three steps I made my way into the main room at The Cheetah. Soft blue smoke and a wide array of colored strobe lights created a halo effect around all of the guests. The place was crowded and lively, but not stuffed to gills like I had seen it in the past. It was a wide rectangular room with a long narrow runway stage at the center with soft leather chairs right up on the rail to ensure the patrons would not miss any of the action nor keep much of a hold on any cash in their pockets. To my right sat a long row of plush couches with velvet ropes and coolers for private parties. On the opposite side of the stage ran a half wall guarded by bouncers reminding the more touchy recipients of lap dances to mind their manners. The bar ran the length of the back wall and an orange neon sign tucked above a door in the corner screamed the entrance to the infamous Champagne Room.

I threw a subtle nod to the deejay that was stationed on a platform that sat above the action. His name was Carl Burke but he went with the moniker DJ Takeoff. He was tall and lanky with the biggest ears you've ever laid eyes on. I never asked him outright but I assumed that the fear of a gust of wind carrying him into the air was where he got his name. Takeoff was a good kid and had proved a reliable asset to me throughout the years.

"Coming to the stage, Chanel. C'mon now put your hands together for Chanel. Y'all in for a real treat," Takeoff said smoothly into his microphone.

I found an empty chair near the far end of the room and slid up to the sticky edge of the stage. Digging through my pockets I came up with a slightly worn out pile of dollar bills and set them in front of me. I was dutifully playing my part, as it was all part of the job.

The bass thudded from overhead speakers sending a soft tingle that started in my feet and traveled to the top of my head. As Chanel plied her trade and made the rounds I scanned the room looking for someone who might be my guy. I had a name and a general description but without a picture my scope was narrowed down to about ten people.

Wheels, also known by his birth name of Clarence Carter appeared at my door in the usual manner, in a small envelope. Once or twice a month these tiny parcels would find their way under my door with a note, neatly typed, containing a name, nickname or any aliases as well as last known locations and known associates. Sometimes a photo would find its way with the note. Photos make it easier.

To call Chanel impressive would have been an understatement. Not only was she a dead knockout but also her stage presence was that of someone more classically trained. Her upper body strength was on full display as she ascended the brass pole at center stage and contorted her body at such extreme angles it made my stomach flip.

As I admired the acrobatics and wondered what the story could be that brought a woman like Chanel to a place like The Cheetah, a pair of slender hands slid down from my shoulders into my chest engulfing me in a gentle bear hug. A small black dagger tattooed on the right forefinger was fading due to age and camouflaged by deep mahogany skin.

"How about you buy me a drink?" the voice said. Her breath was tinged with menthol cigarettes and the slight stench of perfume and sweat hit my nose.

"How about you buy me a drink? You girls seem to be the ones with all the money in this place," I said.

"You know that's not how this works, baby."

"Can't fault me for tryin'."

"Come with me."

I got up from my chair, grabbed the pile of singles from the stage and tossed them forward. It was fair contribution for Chanel's exhilarating performance. She caught this gesture from the corner of her eye and feigned a frown that she wouldn't get to me personally but I blew her a kiss and she caught it with a long lashed wink of her eye.

I ambled up to the bar, managed to flag down a bartender

and ordered a double gin and tonic with no ice and a whiskey and soda. I paid for the drinks and handed the whiskey off to Ms. Dagger Hand.

"How you been, Evelyn?" I asked.

"Boy, keep your voice down. Inside these walls, I am the fabulous Ms. Cocoa Brown."

"Cocoa Brown, huh? Sounds like the title of a badass 70's movie."

"Yeah, well, when every guy wants to know your real name you need to come up with some badass shit."

I knew firsthand that Evelyn Greene was indeed one bad momma. I've know her since I first came to Harbor Point and rented a crumbling one-bedroom above the Chinese joint down on Atlantic Avenue. There were two units upstairs and Evelyn occupied the other with her then boyfriend, Malcolm. Through no fault of her own, various domestic issues compelled me to lend a hand and extricate Malcolm from the premises and ensure he would never return. Since then anytime I needed something I sought out Evelyn first. She was born here, never left and knows everything about everyone and if she didn't, she could connect me with someone who did.

As I watched her sip the whiskey and soda, the expression on her face told me that she had what I needed.

"Wheels. The getaway driver. Been flashin' a ton of cash around and it seems that some people ain't too happy about it and here you are, " Cocoa Brown said in between sips.

"Here I am," I said as I raised my glass.

I finished my drink with a long deep gulp and slid the empty glass to the edge of the bar. I raised a finger indicating to the barker that I was in need of another. I am not a drinker, never have been. When on the job I tend to indulge because it dulls the edge from the task at hand and allows a sense of fluidity. Only once was it ever a real problem but that was Miami many years ago. It was a different life for me then. As I pushed faded memories of Cuban hitmen from my mind I returned my attention to Cocoa.

"Where is he now?" I said.

"He's in the back. Champagne Room," she said. "But Ellis, be careful, this one's a biggie."

Ellis. She doesn't call me by my given name often, as it's usually an assortment of cutsie nicknames like sugar and baby. For a while and for a reason I still can't figure out, it was muffin. The use of my name indicated to me her seriousness. I decided to leave the second gin and tonic on the bar. There would be time for that later.

"Take me back?" I asked.

"Sure."

She grabbed my hand and I followed her to the door under the neon sign. We crossed through into another wide expanse of a room that was lined along the edges with a number of private rooms with red curtains closing them off to prying eyes. Two bouncers as big as Reggie stood on opposite sides of the room. A noble profession no doubt, the Stripper Sentry. A circular couch sprawled across the center of the room. Four young women were occupied with a customer. Booze bottles and piles of cash littered the floor at their feet. They took turns grinding, shaking and rubbing themselves all over his body.

"That's him," Coca said.

She led me to opposite side of the couch and I sat down essentially back-to-back with Wheels. Cocoa climbed on top of me and proceeded to go through the motions of a lap dance. It was good but it wasn't supposed to be. We had slept together once, a few months after she was newly single. She was lonely and I was there but it never happened again and I hadn't really thought about it again until now.

She leaned her head against mine and whispered, "What's the plan, genius?"

I was still working that one out. For some, honesty is the best policy. You just walk up, announce your intentions and if they refuse to come peacefully then you accommodate them and force their understanding of your position. But Wheels was big and mean, at least he looked mean. He was also drinking and that made anyone unpredictable. The two bouncers also complicated the matter for me as it could be reasonably inferred that they were armed. Having no weapon put me at a severe disadvantage.

With Cocoa on top of me, I ran the possible scenarios in my head. It occurred to me that I was playing with house money. Wheels was an easy get and now, I knew his face. There was no tailing, questioning, or physical altercations of any kind. It took two phone calls and an overpriced cover charge to find what I was looking for so I did what so many times before I was unable to. I decided to wait. And perhaps I let Cocoa go on grinding a little bit longer before I let her in on it.

I wished I had brought a jacket. It was the end of March and the days were starting to warm up but it could still be bitterly cold before sunrise. As I exited The Cheetah I pulled a cigarette pack from my pocket, searched another for my lighter and lit up, drawing smoke deep into my lungs.

The parking lot was across the street next to a seaside souvenir shop. The type that sold bathing suits, shoddily made embroidered sweatshirts with the words Harbor Point and any number of imported trinkets for tourists to purchase and never look at again. It had been a very long time since this area of the city had been a tourist destination. The boardwalk that ran behind The Cheetah had been abandoned years ago and stood in stark contrast to the city center with its giant Ferris wheel, shops, eateries and amusements. Two miles apart. Different neighborhoods. Different worlds.

It was little after four in the morning when Wheels stumbled out of the club. Cloaked in darkness I watched him as he came towards me with a slight shimmy in his step. A thick gold chain swung from his neck and a flat brimmed black baseball cap rested on his head at a crooked angle. He was whistling to himself and twirling a set of car keys on a finger. For someone who had dangerous people on his tail, he wasn't trying to make himself hard to find.

From the shadows I positioned a half finished cigarette between my thumb and forefinger, took aim and launched the smoldering tobacco into the air. Wheels didn't seem to notice until it hit him directly in the chest, sending burning ash down the front of his shirt.

"What the fuck," he said, stopping dead in his tracks and looking from left to right.

"Hey Clarence," I said. I stepped from the dark and into the overhead glow of a street lamp.

On his face was a mixture of confusion and rage. He wiped his shirt and took steps forward. "You done fucked up," he said, "You know that, right?" A wicked sneer expanded across his mouth.

I put my hands up, palms facing out to indicate I did not want to scuffle. "Interesting. I would say you were the one who fucked up. You got a lot of people out here looking for you, Clarence," I said in a tone of politeness. "Now don't make this any harder than it needs to be."

He halted his advance in my direction and in a crouched position placed both hands on his knees. His laugh was loud and boisterous.

"And who's gonna make it hard for me? You?" He managed to get the words out through his laughing fit. "That has got to be the funniest shit I ever heard in my life."

"You got one more chance, big boy."

"Aight, Ima light yo ass up."

He slipped his keys into his pocket and raised both fists in front of his face. A mistake on his part as I now knew for sure that Wheels wasn't packing. He moved quickly forward starting to bob his head. Wheels was ready to rumble.

"Don't say I didn't warn you," I said. I stepped from the sidewalk and into the middle of the street. It had been a year or so since I had been in the ring and even further removed from boxing professionally. Wheels did have a good five inches on me and certainly a weight advantage and now that I looked at him he may even have had some professional training. So did Edwin Bonafacio. They called him El Matador. That was Atlantic City many years ago. That was a good night.

Much like riding a bike, boxing is a skill that you carry with you for the rest of your life. I flexed my wrists and loosened my shoulders with little hunches and rotations. I got up on the balls of my feet and the easy bounce returned to me. Wheels came forward grinning and I popped two soft left hand jabs into his belly. They were distance-measuring shots not meant to do any real damage. Wheels chuckled to himself as he continued to stalk me. I circled and waited for a real opening. I saw it coming before he threw it. His shoulder twitched and uncoiled what would have been a devastating right hook. I instinctively crouched at the waist and slid my head under his arm. When a fist lands dead center on the kidney it can cripple a man and unfortunately for Wheels I knew exactly where to locate it. My left hand detonated on his lower back sending a small shockwave through his body. I could hear the small grunt Wheels released through now clenched teeth. As he hit the pavement his legs flailed back and forth while his hand tried to massage out the pain. That wouldn't be enough for him.

I grabbed his shoulder and rolled him flat onto his back.

He moaned a deep sorrowful moan. He was writhing in pain but this was no time for sympathy or apologies. I stuck two short successive right hands into his face and put Wheels to sleep.

Easy enough. All that was needed now was a small forklift to get this pile of dead weight into my car. I looked back across the street and saw Reggie leaning against the wall of the club watching me. He had witnessed the whole thing and did not interfere. That was good enough for me and I decided to try my luck.

After rolling Wheels into the gutter to safeguard someone from running him over I jogged the hundred or so feet to the entrance of The Cheetah.

Reggie looked down at me expressionless. "I knew I seen you before," he said.

"We can take a photo later but I gotta ask you for a quick favor?"

CHAPTER TWO

THE DRIVE UP TO VICTORY CITY WAS FORTY MINUTES. After Wheels was delivered to his final destination, it was another twenty-minute bus ride to the airport where I picked up my car from the long-term parking lot. I never took my personal ride on a job.

It was a long night and by the time I arrived home, pulling my 1985 Cutlass Supreme into the alley below my apartment, I could see that Omar Ruiz was already hard at work. Through the grimy windshield I could see Omar unloading fresh vegetables from the back of his van. The Ruiz family had opened La Superiora Taqueria many years ago and I had the good fortune of living above a slice of taco heaven for three of those years. On a normal day Omar and I would have exchanged pleasantries, I may have asked about his family and business. Before long, I would be in the kitchen chowing on a breakfast burrito or some day-old tamale made by Omar's mother, Inez. But I was tired and the only criticism I could level at Omar was that he was too friendly and did not even remotely understand the simple neighborly head-nod agreement of so many

Americans. I waited for Omar to fill his arms with an oversized cardboard box filled with leafy green lettuce to make my move.

I killed the ignition. Then carefully opened the door so as not to hit the brick wall and slid myself out into the alleyway. It was still dark but it was morning and it had become very cold. My breath hung a cool white vapor trail in the air. The gravel crunched beneath my feet as I made my way to the back of the building. Turning the corner I moved quickly to a long metal staircase that ran up to the second floor. Catlike, I took the steps two at a time until I was out of sight on the balcony above. Quietly tiptoeing to the door at the edge of the balcony I could hear Omar making the return to his truck. He was carrying a soft tune in a language I never could learn or understand but it was sweet and beautiful and I felt a pang of guilt for avoiding him: not enough to carry me back downstairs but guilt nonetheless. It was these moments when I was reminded that I might after all still be a human being. It was an easy justification in my mind for the last twenty-four hours where searching, assaulting, and capturing a man was all in a days work. Not to mention the transport and drop off where the fate of Wheels was out of my control. I slid my key into the lock, turned the knob in one fluid motion, and entered into the kitchen, shutting the door behind me.

The smell of sweet eucalyptus and tobacco hit my nose and sent warning bells blaring in my mind. It was the smell of nostalgia, of better days ahead, and a carefree attitude that I had almost forgotten about. There was also a hint of danger in the air.

Everything in the kitchen was in order including the two day old pile of dishes that rested in the sink.

I moved into the living room. It was a bare space with a

garage sale couch, a rectangular wooden coffee table that Boris too often used as his own personal scratch post, and a cloth covered lazy boy recliner that was here when I moved in. There was a front door attached to the living room and even in the dark I could see the dead bolt was unlocked which confirmed my suspicion. I was frozen. Not with fear but with apprehension. I hoped it wasn't true but I felt pretty confident about what was waiting for me in the next room.

Past a small bathroom and down a narrow corridor I made my way to the bedroom door that was cracked open, allowing the first glimpse of daylight to spill onto the hallway floor. I extended a hand and gave the hollow core door a nudge with my fingers. It swung forward, creaking as it went until it came to rest against the inner wall.

She sat cross-legged in my favorite leather chair. Boris, nestled in her lap, raised an eye and barely acknowledged me as a soft meow croaked from his mouth. He always liked her better.

We stared at each other through the waning darkness and I did not breathe or move a muscle. I was locked in a mental wrestling match. There was a burning urge to kiss her deeply and take her to bed, but also a yearning to choke the life from her and bury her deep in the marshes. Perhaps aware of this struggle she spoke first.

"Ellis Boone. Still haven't changed those locks, huh?"

The smooth pitch and soft delivery of her voice was disarming but I was resolute and determined not to crumble as I had so many times before. I stood still, expressionless.

"I'm glad you didn't. Was cold last night," she continued.

"I know a guy who can take care of it for me."

"Don't be mean now."

Boris raised himself up, arched his back into a deep, full stretch, and leapt from the chair. He did two figure eights between my legs and disappeared. A moment passed before the tearing of wood under his claws could be heard in the living room.

The morning light was now rushing through the open blinds and I was able to get my first real look at Cheriqui Daniels in over three years. I never called her by her given name. To me, she was just, Cherry. The last time I gazed into those eyes we kissed softly, rolled over and went to bed. Then she was gone.

She was exactly as I remembered. Height wise she was small but her physical stature and posture spoke to something much more solid and voracious. Her perfectly round hair added a good six to seven inches to her height as well. She possessed a perfect button nose which sat in line above a long set of lips that brought back memories of an infectious, deep laugh which had an enlightening effect on everyone who encountered it. She was curvaceous in all the right places and was a sight to see when she unleashed herself on anyone who underestimated her. Cherry knew who she was and was keenly aware that sometimes to survive in this city, a game had to be played. Was it fair? No, but she usually figured out a way to walk away unscathed. All of this fire she possessed, both physically and mentally, was encased in a dark brown coating the color of the finest Dutch chocolate. Each step she took sent me right back to that first moment I laid eyes on her.

She got very close to me in the doorway. "You deserve everything I give you," I said, trying not to look her directly in the eyes.

"There's no reason to be like that Ellis," she said as she brushed her hand on my shoulder. She maneuvered herself around me and made her way into the living room. "After all, today is your lucky day."

I entered the bathroom and locked the door behind me, something I had never done in the three years I had lived in the apartment. Like everything else the bathroom was sparse. With no need for privacy a clear shower curtain hung from a steel metal pole with what was supposed to be white suction cups at either end but were now speckled brown from lack of cleaning. The sink was no better; a soft and faded tan ring ran the circular length inside the porcelain sink. On the wall was a mirror that was in major need of a coat of Windex and as I stared at myself through the dried water spots I thought that this must be some kind of sleep deprived nightmare and that when I opened the door she would be gone.

With two fingers I gripped the bottom edge of the mirror and yanked a bit until it swung toward me, revealing the medicine cabinet. There was an over rolled tube of toothpaste, a prescription for some unpronounceable antibiotic that had long since passed the expiration date and a plain bottle of aspirin with no label. It was amazing to notice all the intricate details of a room I had been in a thousand times before. The pounding behind my eyes that had started in the bedroom had followed me and now sat directly in the center of my forehead with little tentacles of pain venturing to the far reaches of my skull. I was stalling as questions raced through my head. Why was she here? Where did she come from? And most importantly, what did she want? Always protect your weak spots and search for an angle to be played against you. Isn't that what she said that one time?

I grabbed the bottle and shook out four small white pills into my open palm. The water was ice cold as it came spilling from the faucet. I popped the tablets into my mouth, haphazardly threw some water back, and swallowed hard.

When I entered the kitchen I wasn't feeling any better. I was just wet. My neckline was dark with either water or sweat. It didn't matter. I still looked like shit and I knew it. Cherry was sitting at the makeshift card table I had been using. She was smoking a cigarette. The soft smoke swirled around the unventilated room and had me questioning my decision to quit.

"You have no food. Not, you should go shopping but you literally have nothing," she said, dropping the half smoked cigarette into a small cup of water. "I was going to make breakfast but we'll have to settle for the diner or something."

I sat directly across from her and spoke very slowly. "You need to leave. There is no reason for you to be here. I'd like you to leave please." I was trying to stay calm and not put her through the fucking wall.

An indignant look crossed her face. Her eyebrows slumped down as she squinted her eyes at me. Her lips pursed.

"Oh Ellis, grow up baby. What is this mopey dopey shit?" She said, her voice raising an octave or two. "What happened to you?"

She got up and crossed the room and placed the palms of her hands on my chest. "I need your help, Ellis, please, just hear me out and if you don't like what I have to say then I'll walk away and you won't never see me again. But I need you to at least hear me," she said softly. "Now please, grab a jacket or something because I need some fucking pancakes."

CHAPTER THREE

You could get decent grub in most neighborhoods. From the dingy joints down in The Bottoms to the more sanitized tourist offerings in the Atlantic Circle, and all the way to the posh spots up on Plantation Hill. For my money there was only one place to consider if you wanted a good breakfast in Harbor Point: Karen's Home-style Kitchen. I navigated the empty side streets running parallel to Atlantic Avenue and I suddenly became very hungry. Cherry and I did not speak during the eight-minute ride from my apartment to the restaurant but a lot can be said with silence. The shock of her return had me in knots but as my stomach began to take over the thought of fried eggs and greasy bacon calmed my nerves.

Walking into Karen's was an overload to the olfactory senses. The smell of freshly brewed coffee mixed with frying sausages multiplied my desire to eat til I was sick. A woman behind the counter called to us as the door closed, "Go on and grab a seat anywhere you like." Cherry led the way past a long counter with stools that faced a giant glass case filled with pies and cakes to a booth in the back big enough to seat six. We slid in opposite each other and I wrestled my sweatshirt over my head.

"You look skinny," she said.

I was trying to think of a smart-ass reply until Rose, an aging redhead wearing a lime green top and black pants appeared holding menus. We made it easy on our waitress by ordering coffees, pancakes, fried eggs, bacon and toast. No menus needed.

"You gonna tell me what this is all about?" I barked.

Cherry leaned in close, reached across the table and took my hands in hers. "I know you hate me. I deserve every ounce of it. Shit, I don't feel so great about me most of the time either and I promise one day I'll explain everything to you but I need you to listen to me very carefully," she said, squeezing my fingers on each syllable that fell from her mouth. She lowered her voice to a whisper. "What if I was to say that I need your help and that you're the only one I can trust and that if you could just be cool for a little while there is money and lots of it buried in the ground not too far from here."

She released her grip and leaned back in the booth. As Rose delivered our steaming cups of Joe, Cherry's eyes bore into my soul. She did not move. She did not blink. She did not thank Rose when she extracted extra sugar packets and placed them on the table. I could have taken a hundred cracks at the reason Cherry was suddenly back in town and in my apartment and now eating breakfast with me but buried treasure would not have been on that list.

I ate my eggs in silence, sopping up the canary yellow yolks with my toast. It was exceptional as always. Cherry moved through her golden brown pancakes like a pro, slicing off hunks with her fork and dropping in extra syrup when needed. Her eyes were focused on her plate as she ate, looking up only occasionally to check my face for clues. As she raised the last bite to her mouth I could see her focus was slightly beyond me to a distance over my shoulder. The fork hung in mid air, frozen.

"We have to go," she said.

I instinctively turned my head in an attempt to pinpoint what exactly she was looking at and saw nothing out of the ordinary. An old man was watching the wall mounted television from the counter. Rose was taking an order from a young lady trying desperately to wrangle a toddler into his high chair and what appeared to be a balding middle aged man with his back to me was reading a newspaper.

"Here's what I'm gonna do," she commanded, refocusing my attention. "I am going to go the bathroom. If Newspaper Man there does anything you come in after me."

She popped out of the booth before I could respond. I thought about leaving her in the bathroom. Just get up, drop some cash on the table, get in the car and head home. The thing about the money in the ground certainly sounded like her. It was like the time her sister was having an affair with a big shot antique coin dealer and she heard about blah, blah, blah, and the next thing I knew I had scuba gear on my back and was getting ready to dive into the Atlantic Ocean off the coast of Georgia. But she delivered, said the money would be there and it was. Perhaps this was like that.

A good five minutes had ticked by and I occasionally eyeballed the Newspaper Man from a long, room length mirror that ran along the back wall of the dining room. I sipped a freshly topped off coffee and watched the balding man. With every turn, the sound of the newspaper pages rustled, sending a sonic spike through my ear and down my spine. I hated that sound.

I drained my coffee cup and reached into my pocket. Rose's service exceeded the standard twenty percent tip and as I felt around in my pocket for the small half fold of bills something caught the corner of my eye. Newspaper Man had risen to his feet and was shuffling off to the bathroom, newspaper neatly folded under one arm. My eyes followed him in the mirror. He kept his gaze mostly focused on the floor but as he made the turn to enter under an open doorway, I caught a look. He tried to conceal it but there was definitely a purposeful glance shot in my direction. My pulse immediately quickened. The adrenaline took over much like before a big fight. It was a strange sensation both exciting and terrifying at the same time. I let out a small exhale, focused myself and waited for the Newspaper Man to disappear under a sign that said, "Little Boys & Girls."

I jettisoned myself from the booth and took large quick strides towards the restrooms, cracking my knuckles and neck as I went. The hallway was dark. There was a matte black door with a silver handle and a rectangular red sign that said "Men." To my immediate left and further ahead, about twenty feet directly in front of me, was another identical black door with a silver handle and a red sign. No sound could be heard except for the muffled voices and clashing of dishes from the kitchen, which must have been on the other side of the wall. I moved toward the ladies room and listened for Cherry's voice. I extended my hand, gripped the handle and entered.

The bathroom appeared empty. A white sink jutted from the

tile and was positioned next to the toilet stall. If it weren't for Cherry's large Afro that crept just above the stall divider I would not have known she was there. Unless he was hiding in the tampon dispenser or the garbage can there was no sign of the Newspaper Man.

"I can see you," I said.

Her feet came into view as she hopped off the toilet seat. She exited the stall and came around the corner to face me. I expected Cherry to be shaken or nervous at the very least but she was a rock. Her forehead creased in deep thought. "I guess I'm just paranoid is all," she said. "Thought I recognized that dude."

"What are you mixed up in?" I demanded.

A loud squeaking noise exploded into the air as the door swung inward violently, almost smashing into my back. I pushed Cherry to the back wall and spun, fists at the ready. Rose looked as shocked to see me as I was to see her. She looked from Cherry's face to mine and slowly backed away. Without a word she turned and exited the bathroom. We waited until the door clicked closed before bursting into laughter.

I gave Cherry some money and sent her up front to handle the check as I headed to the men's room. I pushed the door open and leaned in about halfway only to hear the rustle of a newspaper from inside the stall.

CHAPTER FOUR

I PRESSED THE GAS PEDAL HALFWAY TO THE FLOOR
and the Cutlass pitched forward, accelerating onto a wide three-
lane freeway just ahead of a speeding tractor-trailer. I clicked the
blinker and moved into the middle lane and let the eighteen-
wheel monstrosity pass me on the right.

It had warmed significantly since the early morning hours
and both Cherry and I cracked our windows. The rushing air
vibrated the glass on both sides and created a wind tunnel effect
with cooler air bringing down the temperature in the
sun-baked car.

"Drive out to Steelhaven," she said, leaning in and elevating
the volume of her voice to ensure I heard her. The Steelhaven
exit was about twenty-five miles northwest of town so as we
cruised I switched on the radio. The local hip hop station, HITZ
109.9, came to life spreading smooth bass through the speakers.
Cherry lit a cigarette and nodded her head in time with the beat.
The tobacco smoke hit my nose and I didn't think twice. I
extended two fingers toward Cherry and asked her to pass the

smoke. I increased the speed of the Cutlass and let the music wash over us as we weaved in and out of traffic.

Steelhaven predated Harbor Point by about forty years. It was originally settled by Eastern European farmers and craftsmen a few hundred years ago and became the cultural and economic center of the region. There were many ethnicities and industries that dominated Steelhaven at one time or another but the one relic that remained was the giant blast furnaces of the old steel mill. Purchased by the city more than twenty years ago it has been turned into public gathering space and a fledgling arts center.

As I directed us through the old sections of town you could still see some remnants of the European influence. The marble fountain for instance, was built by Balkan steel mill workers in their spare time as a place to congregate and pass local gossip. Now, it sat derelict at the center of Kane Park where although there are no Balkans left to visit with, it stands as a stark reminder of the rich history of the area.

"Make a left here. At the end of the block make another left," Cherry directed.

We were in an upper class neighborhood called Inferno Point. Big colonial houses with picket fences, pristine lawns and giant swimming pools.

I turned onto Sycamore Street marveling at how the other half lived. It wasn't a feeling of envy but every time I went through neighborhoods like that one I felt a quick jolt of regret, that I did something wrong along the way and a couple of different decisions could have landed me in one of those big houses.

"Here. Pull over," she said.

I pulled up next to the curb and switched off the engine.

"Where am I supposed to be looking?" I asked as my eyes swept up and down the street.

"That one there, two up with the sign."

Halfway up the block sat a massive house consisting of three stories and many windows. The door was red as were the shutters. A paved path ran from the front brick porch and wound along to the right of the house and the driveway that connected to a three bay detached garage. A rusty basketball backboard and hoop with no net sat neglected at one end of the blacktop. The landscaping was overgrown and there were no cars in the driveway. A yellow For Sale sign was planted at the edge of the lawn nearest the road.

"We buying a house?" I asked.

"The name Andrew or Cathy Kramer mean anything to you?"

I conducted a cursory search of my memory banks. "No, I don't think so. Should it?"

"If you were someone who actually owned a television or read the paper or oh…I don't know, lived on the planet with the rest of us, yeah maybe it would."

"Livin' in your world isn't good for me. Safer in my own system."

She dismissed me with a wave of her hand.

"Anyway, Kramer—"

It came to me all at once. "Baseball player right? Played for the O's? Or was it The Bombers?"

"Close. No dipshit. Kramer ran the local funeral home. Fourth generation mortician."

"And why should I know anything about him?"

"A few years back Kramer hired a hit man to kill his wife. Guy broke into that house right there while she was home alone, cornered her in the bathroom and shot her four times."

As Cherry talked I watched the house intently, picturing a figure clad completely in black stalking a woman in a skimpy white negligee. She tried to run but kept falling until he raised the gun. It felt like so many bad cable movies I watched as a kid.

"Are you even listening to me Ellis? Damn!" she snapped.

"I'm listening. Just trying to visualize it."

"Can I continue?"

I waved her on with a flick of my wrist.

She sighed and lit a cigarette. "Anyway she gets it like four times in the back. Blood everywhere and she's not moving. The shooter moves through the house, stages a burglary like he's told from the husband and leaves."

"Easy enough."

"Kramer pays him ten thousand bucks."

"You get what you pay for."

"So Kramer makes two big mistakes. One: about a week and a half before the thing goes down, he issues an additional insurance policy on his wife. Two: an undercover agent sees Kramer in The Bottoms outside of Charley's two days after the murder with a duffle bag over his arm."

"Genius."

"It's not too long before the cops pick up the shooter and he rolls over. Kramer faces indictment, refuses to deal and takes it all the way to trial."

"That's a rocket ship to death row if you ask me."

"Not quite. Twenty-five to life. He's been up there for almost two years."

It was a suburban tragedy and I guess I felt bad but I wasn't getting how this related to Cherry or myself. But I was curious.

"What happened to the wife?" I said.

"I'm going to show you," she said as she tossed her cigarette out the window.

We parked the car just inside the open gate of the Steelhaven Cemetery. Little gray dots littered the distance with a blurred mixture of vibrant red and blue; headstones and American flags.

The wind had picked up and I grabbed a hoodie from the trunk. Cherry led the way and as we walked through the land of the dead. I still couldn't figure this thing out. She reappears after how many years talking about life insurance policies, hit men and dead wives. My meter for detecting bullshit was usually a fine tuned machine but with Cherry I always had a hard time. It was impossible to tell if she was lying or even exaggerating slightly so I decided to follow the tale and see if I liked the ending.

We reached the summit of a small incline and the grass immediately rolled downhill. More tombstones continued in neat little rows until the cemetery boundary ended at a road about three hundred yards from where we stood.

"You see that?" She said, pointing into the distance toward a white building that was across the road.

"Yeah. What is it?" I said.

"That is Meyer Funeral Services."

"Good location."

"Formerly Kramer Funeral Home."

"Oh," I said, still trying to piece the puzzle together. I realized Cherry was only handing out enough to progress a little at a time, withholding in certain spots, giving me just enough to keep me interested. "Where's the wife buried?"

"That's the thing. She didn't die in that bathroom."

"Why did Kramer pay for the shooter then?"

Cherry motioned for me to follow her and we started down the hill.

"The guy stages the burglary, right? Keep in mind, it's the middle of the day so when he leaves the house a neighbor see him, knows something is up and calls the cops," she says as we turn down a row to the left. "The cops find her but she isn't dead. Crazy enough she's not even that seriously hurt, ya know, except for all the holes but the bullets missed all vital organs and she just lost a lot of blood."

"Lucky bird," I said, trying to keep up.

"She comes to at the hospital and tells the detectives that it was one hundred percent her husband that tried to have her killed. The cops and doctors decide to keep her isolated while they figure it out. One of the jakes, on his way out of the hospital goes to the husband and gives his condolences, just to see how he would react. The husband takes that as confirmation that his wife is dead and he proceeds to basically put himself in prison with all the dumb shit he does after that."

"How do you know all this?" I asked.

"I'm getting there. So Kramer gets arrested. And you can only imagine his face when the detectives tell him his wife is alive but he stands firm. He goes down. She divorces him immediately after the verdict. Then takes her maiden name and assumes control over the funeral home."

I have questions upon questions but the one that rolled out of my mouth was:

"How was she so sure he was behind it?"

"She threatened to expose him to the cops and he, in turn, said he would kill her if that ever happened. I guess he got paranoid because as far as I know she never went to the cops."

"What was Kramer into?"

""Distributing, gun running, money laundering. You name it. Mostly for The Celestials but maybe for bigger fish too."

"Bikers? Jesus."

"He was using the coffins, the furnaces, everything at his disposal. Fancied himself a gangster of sorts."

Cherry had come to a stop and was looking down at an intricate headstone carved in the image of an angel. It had flowers at the base. I felt a feeling of overwhelming sadness looking at the decaying petals against the cold marble and brown grass. A feeling of exhaustion erupted inside me and rushed at full speed toward my head.

"That's a great story but," I said. I turned and grabbed her by the shoulders. "What the fuck does this have to do with you or me? Cut to it already. I'm sick of the breadcrumb dropping."

She smiled and shot a thumb over her shoulder toward the white building across the road. "Because I am the fairly new personal assistant to the former Mrs. Kramer now Ms. Meyer."

"Congratulations. Good for you. I'm going back to the car." I threw up my hands, exasperated as I turned from her.

"Listen to me, wait, stop," she pleaded, reaching for my arm. "Come here."

I took the two strides and stood next to her. I felt defeated. I just wanted to go home, curl up with Boris and sleep for a day or two. Cherry tended to do that to me.

She pointed down at the angelic headstone.

"This woman, right here. I want to imagine that she worked her whole life and hopefully at the end of that life she didn't regret anything. She picked out the perfect plot on a little hill in the town she grew up in. She prepaid for the services and as her life drew to a close that planning gave her comfort. Her family was with her when she took her last breath and they had a lovely ceremony." She grabbed my elbow and squeezed. "We should all be so lucky."

I closed my eyes and envisioned the end of my own life. It was not pretty.

"There's only one problem. I'm pretty sure that the coffin buried beneath our feet doesn't have any human remains in it. If I'm right, and I think I am, then we are standing on twenty five-million dollars."

I opened my eyes and looked into hers. "And I need your help to dig it up."

CHAPTER FIVE

Boris was a basket case by the time I arrived back at home. Everything that was on the counter had been knocked to the floor in a spiteful action that was at the core of Boris's character. The guttural sound that emanated from his mouth was more akin to feline torture than the smooth and sometime operatic tones that I had become accustomed to over the years.

When I finally got around to ripping open a can of tuna and dropping it in the usual spot, Boris's delirium was at a fever pitch. Once the wet food touched his mouth, he engrossed himself in the tiny can allowing for a sense of calm to once again return to the apartment.

I needed a shower and a stiff drink but my exhaustion would only allow for one. I chose the shower. The hot water felt like an awakening on my skin. I scrubbed the previous days activities from my body, washed my hair with some cheap stuff from the corner store and relieved myself down the drain. It was a bad habit I had fallen into but I figured fuck it, what's a little piss on your feet in the shower? I brushed my teeth vigorously until my spit was a pinkish mixture of blood and toothpaste and gargled with a cheap brown mouthwash. I hit the bed naked, ready to pass into the oblivion of sleep.

But the sweet peach of a dream state never materialized. It had been less than twenty-four hours since my run in with Wheels at The Cheetah and I was looking forward to a couple of days off the street. Then Cherry showed up and blew everything to shit. I had dropped her off at a friend's house downtown and was sure to get my key from her. It's not that I lacked trust but I was not comfortable with an open door policy with anyone at this point.

Almost any form of physical punishment is preferable when sleep will not come. I tossed and turned, tried to lay completely still, jerked off, and even counted fucking sheep. None of it worked because my mind kept drifting back to the money. The amount Cherry had teased was the carrot that might get me out of Harbor Point for good. No more chasing down guys slightly worse than me in The Bottoms or late night drives to abandoned warehouses out in Greenfield. No more burner phones or money drops. No more decoy license plates and airport vehicle swaps. I was intrigued, even enticed but optimism in any relationship to "the one big score" was a cruel mistress that I did not plan on bedding down again.

That hopefulness for the big payday, that one job that will set you up for life and see you off with a boat and a margarita in the Caribbean can drive you insane and put you in the clink for stretches that turn even the hardest men soft. That was not in the cards for me. It happened once and I took my shot at the prize and came up short. I am lucky to be alive. That time wasn't totally Cherry's fault but when I think back on the mistakes that were made, it kinda was.

I got up from the bed and flicked on the overhead fan praying that a spat of cool air would do the trick. I rolled onto my side and began to doze off. As my eyes closed I could feel Boris hop onto the bed and curl up around my knees.

My dreams were typically not memorable. Only a handful since high school are easily recalled. Most evaporate into the ether as soon as my eyes open but the dream I had the day Cherry came back into my life will, I fear, be with me for longer than I'd like. A series of flashes, muzzle flashes maybe, seared into my subconscious with a combination of graveyard zombies, piles of burning cash and cadavers standing upright, walking themselves to the incinerator.

I woke up with a deep gasp, desperately trying to fill my lungs with air. Boris shot off the bed and out of the room. Sweat poured from my forehead and my sheets were soaked. The tan sheets had turned a deep, dark brown.

The sun had set and the bedroom was dark. I dressed in sweatpants and a bulky hoodie and searched for my sneakers in the back of the closet.

It must have rained while I slept as Filmore Street, the road that ran in front of La Superiora Taqueria was slick and carried the yellow and green reflection from the neon sign that hung above the storefront.

I needed to clear my head. My feet started slow, walking at first but before I had gone two blocks I was up to a light jog. The plan was to carry me down Filmore all the way to the boardwalk then along the oceanfront til I hit the border for the Atlantic Circle neighborhood where a slant up Greyson Boulevard would bring me up to the main thoroughfare, Atlantic Avenue. From there it would be a straight shot back to Filmore. Six miles.

My route started out perfectly fine but began to wobble before I had the boardwalk in sight. I picked up the tail the moment my legs began their acceleration. The boardwalk came into view and I abruptly changed direction. I crossed the wet pavement and shot into an alleyway between Art's Bakery and 3rd Eye Tattoos. I located two large plastic recycling bins along the brick wall and concealed myself behind their girth. There was nothing at first, save for the warm air escaping my mouth, leaving a mist hanging in front of my face. The squeal of wet brake pads gave away the vehicle before it rolled into sight. Between the cans I could see the front end creep by until the passenger door and window came into view.

"Shit," I said to no one in particular.

Through the rain-streaked window, behind the wheel I glimpsed a middle aged balding man. It was Newspaper Man.

My knees started to tingle as I tried to do my best statue imitation. The Newspaper Man scanned the alleyway for another minute or so before he took his foot off the brakes and let the car drift forward and ultimately out of my sight. I got up, flexed my hamstrings a bit and made my way through the back lots of businesses that ran along Filmore. There weren't many residences left along the avenue and those that did exist were second floor jobs like mine, usually above a store of some kind. There were two fences and three dogs I had to navigate before I came out onto Hatfield Street, which crossed Filmore at the corner. To my right and up a block or so I could see the lights from The Taqueria. I flipped up my hood and ran at a solid clip until I was in my own alleyway. There were no headlights on my tail and I saw no sign of the Newspaper Man.

Trying not to draw attention or make a rattle I took the steps one at a time until I was on the landing. Nothing out of place.

Except...

A small brown paper bag sat at the base of the screen door that lead into the kitchen. I reached down and plucked the folds at the top of the bag, lifting it to my side. The smell gave the contents away and I was relieved.

Inside, I shared my tacos, rice, beans and masa with Boris who, quite predictably, acted as if he was starving to death as I came in the door. I would not see it until much later, but while Boris and I consumed our dinner, a medium sized manila envelope slipped under the front door.

CHAPTER SIX

SHE LOOKED LIKE SHE WAS FIFTEEN TOPS WITH A messy bun tied atop her head and dull brown eyes that gave the impression of either contempt or indifference. Maybe the photograph was old but the girl in it could not have been far removed from middle school. On the back of the inkjet printed photo was the name Alana Cruz scrawled in barely legible faded pencil. Underneath the name was an address and two business names. The first, Up Down Left Right, was an arcade on the boardwalk in the heart of the Atlantic Circle, directly across from the Ferris wheel and a popular hangout for locals before the crush of the summer tourist season. The second, Snack Attack was a typical late night grease stand for the inebriated to soak up the undigested alcohol in their bellies. It too was located along the boardwalk in close proximity to the more mainstream attractions.

The address listed was in The Pearl, a four square block grid beyond The Bottoms, where even the Harbor Point police were reluctant to venture. It survived on its own code of justice and with a particular brand of violence. A few times a year severed hands would find their way onto the front page of the papers reminding the rest of the region that The Pearl was an actual place. In my experience most of the street drugs that made it into Harbor Point came through a handful of individuals in The Pearl.

That's how it usually happened. A name, which may or may not be accurate, a photo, maybe a few spots where the target might have been seen and a last known address. Easy right? As I sat on the couch drinking a black coffee I invented a story that might make this young girl seem like a monster. It was all part of a routine I had devised to prepare myself for the days activities because once I left the house it really didn't matter what she did or did not do. This was how I chose to build my livelihood and it was either them or me. Truth be told I hated this shit more than anything but when the boxing career disappeared due to concussions it became the thing I was most suited for.

I had met the Kreski brothers years before when I was competing in amateur boxing tournaments around the country. Roman was a stable mate of mine at a few national tournaments and we even bunked together during the Olympic trials. His older brother Max was always hanging around, rooting on his brother and assisting in the training when he could. Max worked my corner one night in Toronto when my cut man came down with the flu. I went further and had more success than Roman but unless you win a world title you end up broke and working a day job that can never match the rush of stepping into the ring.

It was a few years ago when Roman approached me at a local

boxing card held at a hotel banquet room off the parkway and asked if I'd like to do some collections. I didn't inquire too much at the time because I desperately needed the money. I was parking cars over at the new Heaven's Gate Casino and it wasn't enough. I was miserable, depressed and looking for anything to make me feel alive again.

The first time I hurt a guy for non-payment was straightforward. His name was Eddie Bozeman. A degenerate gambler who could not understand that parlays were for suckers, was into the brothers for about six grand when they sent me looking for him. He protested, pleaded, cursed me and eventually cried when I broke three of his fingers but within a week he was on a payment plan and to this day has not run afoul again. It gradually progressed from collections to apprehensions and deliveries. It paid the bills and allowed me a certain level of freedom but it didn't feel good and I had been looking for a way out. My mind, as it had over the last few hours, drifted back to Cherry and the graveyard.

I finished my coffee, made sure to feed Boris and headed out into the morning air. Unlike most of the past month the temperature was moderate indicating a warmer day ahead.

I twisted the ignition on the Cutlass and brought her to life. She purred and puttered and I needled her with some gas and until she was warmed up. As I drove downtown I wondered again what I would be doing on a day like this if I didn't have to do what I was doing.

It was far too early and an unlikely time to find Alana Cruz out and about on the streets but I wanted to get the lay of the land and see exactly what I would be dealing with. Both the Up Down Left Right and the Snack Attack were closed up. The boardwalk and surrounding streets were mostly deserted save for the occasional speed walker or amateur photographer taking in the ocean or the empty amusements.

I took Beach Boulevard, which ran along the boardwalk, toward The Bottoms. Three and four story motels with garish colors of pinks and blues dotted the road on either side. Each promised amenities such as free Wi-Fi or HBO on little signboards below names like The Breezeway, The Cozy Palm or Tradewinds. Staples in any city on the beach. It was the same a block over on Atlantic. Come summer time these roads would be jammed, but now, in the morning hours of late March it's a straight shot to my destination with a few stop signs and no lights. Atlantic, however, is full of lights and is to be avoided at any time of year.

When the hotels disappear and the boardwalk falls into disrepair you know what part of town you are entering. It's not only the physical signs but also something in the air. The ocean sounded different. It screamed like a warning signal to out-of-towners to, "Turn Back!" I continued on through The Bottoms and found the address I was looking for on a street lined with old row homes in various states of decrepitude. The one constant in The Pearl, on every railing and from every available window, were the bright red stripes, blue triangles and white stars of the Puerto Rican national flag. There was no mistaking the boundary to this hood and although there was some overlap on Brunson Street, where The Bottoms and The Pearl met, beyond that it was exclusively Boricua.

I parked along the curb two and half blocks from the address I was given. "24 Arlington Place" which the note read on the back of the photo. An old woman, with long gray hair pulled back into a tight ponytail, swept the stoop back and forth in hard, sharp motions. Dust and debris kicked up and clouded the surrounding area. When the haze settled there was no sign of Alana Cruz. It wasn't expected but considering the luck I had tracking Wheels a part of me hoped it would be as easy.

I drove slowly down the street and eyed the open door where the woman was now admiring her handiwork. She turned and eyed me with a certain venom in her stare. My head snapped back to the road just in time to see a young girl with dull brown eyes and a pink backpack in the middle of the crosswalk, frozen. The brakes on the Cutlass screamed as I pressed the pedal hard to the floor, bringing the car to a stop within inches of her body.

Her calm demeanor at almost being flattened by a two thousand pound vehicle was unnerving as I attempted to prevent myself from hyperventilating. I looked at her looking at me, expressionless. Then I saw it. Alana Cruz front and center.

My hands still shaking, I pushed the door open and went to the front of the car. I couldn't think of anything to say but, "You okay?"

The little girl, and she was a little girl, no more than fourteen or fifteen, stared at me with a look of bewilderment across her smooth face. Her eyes darted over my shoulder. She saw it before I felt it.

WHACK! The old lady with the broom applied it without prejudice to my head and neck, screaming at me in Spanish. I didn't speak the language but there were quite a few profanities woven into her onslaught. Spinning to try and grab hold of the handle my feet instinctively carried me backwards toward a parked car that I crashed into sending the blare of an alarm sailing into the air. From the corner of my vision I could see Alana moving through the crosswalk toward the other side of the street. I thought I glimpsed a smile crease her lips as she disappeared around a corner.

The old woman's relentless barrage combined with the car alarm was drawing attention from residents coming to their windows and stoops to see what the commotion was about. I managed to catch the broomstick mid-air and in one swift motion broke it over my knee. The old woman spat at me and began to shuffle back to her porch when two men, one extremely overweight wearing a knit cap and boxer shorts and the other a small man even for small man standards, stepped off the curb and into the street. They approached rapidly.

"Hey yo, what you doin' to my car gringo?" the fat man said.

"You in the wrong neighborhood motherfucker," someone shouted from a window.

I made a move toward my car but the smaller of the two cut me off and shoved me hard in the chest. I was not itching for a fight. Not here.

"Hey listen guys, it was just a big misunder—," A third man, who must have crept around the corner, grabbed me from behind and jammed his forearm under my neck and squeezed. It caught me off guard and I suddenly realized the danger I was in. A jerking motion had me off my feet and on the ground. My hands immediately went to my head as a series of fists and feet were launched on all areas of my body. From my ground level view I saw the driver side door to the Cutlass swing shut and seconds later she was gone.

The rage hit me in the chest first before it exploded to my extremities. My teeth found one of the assailants bare calf muscles and I bit down, sinking into the meaty flesh. This sent him retreating from the fray for a brief moment. A moment was all that I needed. I rolled into the middle of the street narrowly avoiding more kicks aimed at my head. I sprung to my feet and went at the first face that came into my vision. POP, POP. Two speedy left hands followed by a crushing straight right put the tiny man into dreamland. His head crashed into the pavement. The fat man looked at his friend and then at me and then back to his friend. He took a set of keys from his pocket, clicked a button and silenced the alarm. My breath was rapid and the blood in my veins boiled. I stalked forward with both fists raised, ready for war. The fat man glanced at his snoring friend one more time before putting his hand up and retreating.

"Just get the fuck outta here and we'll call it even," he said, slight whine to his voice.

"Even?" I said slowly through clenched teeth.

I could instinctively feel more people on the street watching. It was imperative that I make my escape as I got real close to the fat man. I could smell the fear seeping from his oversized pores. He turned his head away from me and closed his eyes.

There were indeed several groups of people on the street watching, mostly confused, as they had not been present to witness the beginning the melee. A small group slowly making their way toward me. One face in particular stood out to me. He was standing above the crowd on the trunk of car. I recognized him immediately from mug shots I had seen over the years. His name was King Tito and I knew I needed to leave.

I turned from the fat man and sprinted up the street, around the corner and straight from The Pearl until I reached the boardwalk. The seagulls were forming overhead, gliding in and out of the wind swells. I kicked off my sneakers, peeled my ankle socks off and stuffed them in my pockets and made my way to the sand. With each step, my body began to ache and a lump had formed at my hairline. After fifty yards my head was pounding.

I took the beachfront back to land of the living, occasionally allowing the ice-cold ocean water to wash over me while attempting to concoct a plan to get my car back.

CHAPTER SEVEN

BORIS WAS PREDICTABLY STARVING WHEN I ARRIVED home. His cries of hunger tore through my aching skull. I could never gauge his eating schedule or if he was really hungry. Boris wasn't shy and if he thought he could get more, he would certainly ask. Only after his belly was satisfied did I sit down and truly reflect on what had happened. They stole my car. My blood started to percolate once again thinking about the assault, the theft but most of all the stone faced teenager Alana Cruz. What could she be into that would put her into the Kreski brothers' crosshairs? I needed a plan and after a futile search through my brain decided an outsourcing of the problem or at the very least, a consultant was needed.

The bedroom was a mess but I ignored it for the time being while I searched a bottom dresser drawer, moving clothes and an almost never used silver revolver. The old cell phone was wedged in the back corner behind a dusty box of ammunition.

On the dresser a small ceramic dish with tiny imprints of red flowers sat beneath a lamp. Inside were several prepaid SIM cards. I pried the battery clip off the back of the heavily scratched flip phone and inserted the card into the slot. Once the clip was reinserted I flipped open the phone, pressed the power button and waited for the device to boot up.

Navigating to the text message screen I scrolled through a sparse list of contacts until Cherry's name was highlighted. I slowly typed out the words:

NEED TO SEE YOU. COME WHEN YOU CAN.

I paused before I hit send, my thumb hovering over the button. Knowing full well the repercussions, I pressed down and closed the phone before tossing it on the dresser.

The next few hours were occupied with a deep cleaning of the apartment. I started in the bedroom, swapping out the sweat stained sheets for fresh ones before moving on to a thorough scrub of the bathroom. I had to retreat to the balcony a few times to get the smell of bleach from my nostrils. The dishes were finally cleaned and Boris expressed his thanks at a clean litter box by immediately taking a piss and launching specks of the small clumping clay out of his box and onto the floor of the closet. I would handle that another time. That cat can be a real bastard sometimes.

Frustration built as I checked the phone and saw no response from Cherry. Alarm bells were ringing deep in my gut telling me to get away but the prospect of the score was intriguing. Like all the times before, however, the warning signs were less effective when Cherry was around. She was a character flaw that I couldn't quite correct.

I ran through the scenario in my head. An empty coffin,

presumably stuffed with cash with an owner rotting in a cell made for a perfect storm kind of situation. It didn't seem as if the wife was the wiser to what she had sitting across the street in that cemetery. Maybe she didn't care. If my spouse hired a hitter to take me out, the prospect of digging though the past to find out exactly what the son of a bitch was up to might not be too enticing.

Cherry's footsteps could be heard through the window as she came up the back steps. I met her at the door and let her in. She was in a dark gray business suit accented with light silver pinstripes, sporting a bright red blouse and shimmering hoop earrings. I had never seen the corporate-chic Cherry, just the down for anything, jeans and sneakers Cherry. Instinctively I leaned in and popped a kiss on her cheek then immediately felt the heat flush to my cheeks.

She turned, avoiding my eyes, and peeled her jacket from her shoulders.

"Don't. You hungry?" I said.

"I can eat."

We grabbed a small table in the corner of La Superiora Taqueria against the large glass window facing the street. The crowd was sparse and as soon as Omar spotted us from the open kitchen beyond the counter he appointed himself our own personal server. He shook my hand and clapped the other on my shoulder before turning his attention to Cherry.

"Miss Cherry, where you been? Why you no come see me no more, eh? The place is...is...less pretty since you go away," he said with a thick accent, grabbing an empty chair and pulling it up close. Never was an order placed in a swift manner when

Omar was present but no one ever seemed to mind. You felt like he had invited you into his personal kitchen.

Cherry's response was in perfect Spanish. They laughed and exchanged pleasantries that were beyond me. Cherry blew two kisses to either side of Omar's face as he retreated into the kitchen. A moment later he returned with two bottles of Mexican soda and a basket of house made tortilla chips with Mama Inez's ridiculous guacamole.

We ordered rice and beans with our shrimp, beef tongue, and fresh lobster tacos. Omar marched to the kitchen like a soldier heading off to face the enemy.

"So?" Cherry said, clicking her nails one at a time on the laminate tabletop.

"How much? If I'm going to help you I need to know that it's worth it."

Shifting in her chair, Cherry said, "Nothing is exact but we're looking in the neighborhood of twenty five. Maybe a little more. Maybe a little less."

"How do you know?"

"How do I know what?"

"All of it? The amount, the spot, that the money is even in the fucking ground?" As the questions poured from my mouth, I felt the agitation in my tone. I softened a bit and asked, "Where did the money come from Cherry?"

The food arrived and took up all available space on the table. We dug in, leaving the question at hand lingering for a moment. After polishing off a shrimp taco and a small pile of rice and beans, Cherry wiped her hands on a paper napkin.

She said, "The old lady put me in charge of everything day to day. Meeting with clients, coordinating procession routes and transfers."

"Transfers?" I said, as rice dribbled from the corner of my mouth, "Where to?"

"The crematorium. That's where I picked this up. There were names on the transport manifests for cremation."

"For bodies that already had headstones," I blurted out, my brain finally making the connection.

"Ding ding."

"Yeah, okay, I get it but how do you nail it down to one? There could be a bunch of coffins stuffed with cash on that hill."

"That's what I thought but then I got my hands on one of Kramer's personal journals. Inside there's notes, drawings, maps. The whole deal. I do think there are other coffins out there but only one has got the cash in it and that's all I'm concerned about."

"What's in the others?"

"Guns."

"Guns?"

"And drugs."

"And you're absolutely sure about the location on the money?"

"No, not absolutely but it's close. I'm still going through the records to nail it down. I wanted to come to you now so we can move when the time is right."

We sat in silence for the remainder of the meal. Once the table was cleaned and I had polished off a giant ball of frozen vanilla ice cream I said, "Okay, I think I'm in."

Cherry was rolling a cigarette between her fingers back and forth eyeing the front door.

Outside we passed the cigarette between each other. "What is there to think about Ellis? No one knows the money is there. We just gotta scoop it out of the ground," she said.

I leaned my back against Omar's front window and ran through it all again in my mind before I said, "Can't imagine it's easy digging up a grave without getting any heat on you. It's not like we can just roll up with a couple of shovels."

"We've got time, baby. I still have to go through the paperwork and see where the rest of it is. While I'm doing that, you work out the fine print."

The word "baby" didn't catch me as off guard as I thought. My mind was deep in the business of how to move all that dirt and cash as quickly as possible.

"And no one knows about this?" I asked as my encounter with the Newspaper Man bolted through my head. For now I'd keep that all to myself.

"No," she said. There was no hesitation in her delivery, however, she didn't look at me when she said it.

I checked my watch and she noticed. "You got somewhere to be?"

I was about to recount my run in with the boys from The Pearl when three cars slowly turned the corner. It would have been an unnoticeable event save for the loud music coming from each of them. Low rumbling bass with indistinguishable lyrics layered on top. It was a static mess to the airwaves. I could only imagine what it was like for the occupants in those cars.

The first two rolled up and stopped at the curb directly in front of us. The lead car was a slick purple and blue Chevy Caprice, maybe early seventies by the look. The follow up, a midnight blue Impala. Both were equipped with sparkling silver rims and blackout tinted windows. In unison, both cars dropped and came to rest an inch or two above the ground. The music abruptly stopped when the third car, which lagged behind the others, cruised by and came to a stop about a half block away. And there it was; the Cutlass.

The passenger door to the Impala swung open and a pocket of gray smoke escaped into the night sky. King Tito stepped out of the car and on to the curb, examining the surroundings. He was of average height with skin like tanned leather. Black tattoos of various designs and symbols covered most of it. He was slow and deliberate in all his movements and as he approached me I could see the muscles flexing in motion under his skin tight white t-shirt.

When he got close enough he said, in a low gravel-laced voice, "You know me? Know who I am?"

I shot a glance at Cherry before I said, "I know who you are."

King Tito turned to Cherry and said, "Can you give us some privacy?"

"She can stay," I said.

A look of displeasure crossed King Tito's face. Cherry stepped toward the entrance to the restaurant, "No, it's okay. I'll wrap up the food and the bill." With a concerned "What-the-fuck" look on her face, she passed through the glass door.

King Tito motioned to the idling Caprice with the snap of two fingers. The passenger door opened and a tall, lanky kid slid from the back of the car and came ambling towards us. His long arms swung behind his back slightly. He donned a knit cap that sat crooked atop his head.

"This is Alex and he has something to say," King Tito said, motioning Alex to come closer.

With his head to the side and without ever looking in my eyes, Alex said, "I apologize for taking your ride."

"Good," said King Tito. He reached into his pocket and came out with a roll of cash. He peeled off a twenty and passed it to

Alex, telling him something in Spanish. Alex nodded his head and entered the Tacqueria leaving King Tito and I alone on the street.

"You handled some of my boys pretty easy today," he said.

"They had it coming."

"The whole thing was very unfortunate. My boys see a Chico Blanco with my niece in the middle of the street and they went too far. I have corrected that. Your car," he said and pointed up the street.

"That girl was your niece?" I said.

"My brother's daughter, yes. He, unfortunately, will not be home again so she is my responsibility now. You can understand why some of my people act the way they do when it concerns her."

"I get it, but you gotta understand that when people come at me I'm gonna defend myself."

"So we understand each other then?" King Tito cracked a smile as he said this. "One more thing and I'll be gone."

The door to restaurant swung open and Alex came out holding a small brown paper bag. He handed some bills back to King Tito and then retreated to the Caprice, disappearing inside. King Tito watched until the car door was closed before turning his attention back to me.

"What were you doing? Why were you on that street?"

Honesty, at least in part, is the best policy right? That thought passed through my mind as I said, "I was looking for someone."

King Tito cocked his head slightly to the side. "I'll put it to you like this. You have business concerning The Pearl or anybody in it you come to me first. Yes?"

"Sure."

"Because if you enter into my home again without being invited or calling first you will not be dealing with my little ones."

"Sounds fair."

King Tito extended his hand. I took it in mine and shook it. "That's it then," he said.

A question nagged at me. "How'd you know where to find me?" I said.

He released my hand and his body language relaxed considerably. "I saw you fight once. I know who you are."

"Where?"

"Convention Center. Angel Alvarez."

"That was a rough night. Alvarez was a scrappy kid. Good fighter. Heavy hands."

"A little rougher for him though."

"On that night it was."

With that, King Tito nodded his head and walked back to the Impala. He shut the door as the car shimmied and rose up back into the driving position. There was a certain beauty in the low rider and the care that went into them. The black tinted window slowly descended and King Tito addressed me once more.

"I have a piece of advice for you, Mr. Boone. You are working for the wrong people. They'll get you killed."

The Caprice moved first with the Impala closely in tow. They turned at the corner and were out of sight before I heard the distant rumble of their speakers.

CHAPTER EIGHT

"THIS IS WHAT YOU'VE BEEN UP TO? YOU'RE GONNA get yourself hurt Ellis. I'm telling you. Messing around with those guys...they're both fucking crazy," Cherry said as she blew smoke through the small opening from the passenger side window. She wasn't wrong but I was hoping I would be able to stay two steps ahead with enough wiggle room to give myself an exit strategy.

We headed toward the boardwalk in the Atlantic Circle. My desire was to feel the Cutlass out and make sure she was still in tiptop shape. It didn't appear that any damage had been done while in the company of King Tito's minions.

It took twenty minutes to cover the scope of my adventures with the Kreskis, Wheels, and The Cheetah. I told her about Alana Cruz as well as all the other underground and outside the law shit I had been up to the last couple of years. I had never verbalized this much about my personal business with anyone.

Cherry didn't react positively or negatively while she took to chewing on the edge of her thumb. She did this when she was nervous.

"What's in your brain?" I said.

"This complicates shit, Ellis. We are on the edge of something huge and now," she paused while looking for a sequence of satisfactory words. "Now there all these other pieces moving in. Fuckin' Cholo gangsters and psycho, eh, I don't even know what to call those guys.

"Tito is Puerto Rican."

She snapped her head in my direction and said, "What's that gotta do with anything?"

"Cholos are Mexican. Tito is Puerto Rican."

"Oh, I see. Mexican knives different from Puerto Rican ones? They make different kinda slugs in San Juan than they do in Tijuana? Shut the fuck up, Ellis You're avoiding the issue. Where the hell are we going anyway? We just went down this street?"

I had looped around and did a slow drive by of The Snack Attack looking for Alana, the Princess from The Pearl. Who knew? It had certainly complicated things and tactics would have to change but to what extent, I had not figured out. Spinning the wheel, I whipped the Cutlass into a hard U-turn and headed back toward the little burger joint. With the parking lot now on my side I got a better look at some of the patrons ordering and eating from the walk up window. It was not a big space, just enough for a handful of picnic tables and garbage cans. Most of the food was consumed standing up or taken to go. Later in the summer The Attack, as some of the locals called it, would be steady with customers from open to close but now, with the air still cool, there weren't more than ten people loitering around and none of them were Alana.

"We are looking for the kid. You don't wanna come? I'll drop you off," I said pulling to the side of the road. The engine idled after I threw the car into park and turned to her.

I said, "Tell me now but either way I gotta find this girl. I don't know what I'm gonna do when that happens but I need to know why the Kreskis have their fangs aimed in her direction." I was agitated now thinking about the girl with the pink backpack and maybe it was stupid but part of it was the respect that King Tito paid to me. Granted, it was a small gesture that came with a side of threats and violence, but it now created conflict in my head where before none existed.

Cherry tossed a sideways look at me, slowly shaking her head, letting me know she was gonna roll. My guess would be that she was as intrigued with the girl as I was but there was no real way to tell except that Cherry always carried the flag for young girls in bad situations.

"Okay, let's go play some video games," I said and pulled the car from the curb.

We parked in the large public lot a block and a half from the boardwalk. It was a quarter full so I decided to skip the automated payment machine at the end of the gate. The police in Harbor Point were no friends of mine but there were enough problems plaguing the area that parking tickets were not high on the priority list of the HPPD's finest, not for a few weeks at least.

We crossed Atlantic Avenue, passed a deserted miniature golf course that was sectioned off behind a large chain link fence and ascended up a ramp and on to the boardwalk properly.

This is where the action happened for everyone who didn't live here year round. The boardwalk stretched for miles in each direction but if there was a center this would be it. A myriad of smells, mostly with a tinge of fried oil to them, wafted through the air. Bright signs, in every color dotted the landscape advertising everything from souvenir t-shirts to fake tattoos and homemade salt-water taffy. The soft roar of the crashing waves beyond the sandy beach added an underlying drone to match the amusements further inland.

For the preseason it was crowded. People milled about, some inspected the games of chance while others held hands and laughed, heading to unknown destinations. If you weren't really looking or didn't know what to see, it would be easy to misconstrue Harbor Point as a happy place.

We navigated our way through a small group of teenagers eating pizza off orange stained paper plates and entered the Up Down Left Right through one of two large sliding bay doors.

Cherry lightly whacked my arm as we entered the arcade. "What's this chick look like?" she said.

I dug into my back pocket and passed the now wrinkled photo of Alana to her. She examined it quickly, handed it back and waded off into the sea of blinking and flashing screens. Unlike the boardwalk it was not heavily populated as many of the machines stood empty. If Alana was here it shouldn't be too hard to find her.

I moved through rows of claw machines, old school stand up games and slid to the back wall, the whole time examining each of the faces I encountered. It wasn't easy. The lights were dim with a mixture of black light and strobe effects. It was a perverse thought but the Up Down reminded me a little of The Cheetah. I moved toward a cluster of young girls who were not playing but sitting on the edge of a long row of Skeeball machines.

Alana was not among them but one of the girls, a sheepish

looking teen with thick glasses and braces, eyed me up pretty hard. I thought it was suspicious but quickly kicked it from my thoughts. I was by far the oldest person in the arcade so it was understandable that I would get some of those looks. As I turned the corner I managed to sneak a glance at the girls and the girl with the glasses was furiously texting away in her phone.

"You wanna play some Whack-a-Mole? I used to love that thing when I was a kid," Cherry said, approaching from a bank of video poker machines that paid out in tickets instead of money.

"Any luck?" I asked.

"No. A bunch of chicas running around but none of them our girl. What's the move?"

"Follow me."

Heading to the far back corner of the arcade we made our way to the gift counter with its long glass encasements filled with some store crap. Sticky hands, army men, fake plastic spiders were just a sampling of the junk that one could bring home if you pumped enough quarters into the machines and gathered the appropriate amount of tickets. On the wall behind and above the cases were high mounted shelving, filled with the more premium prizes that included statuettes, game systems, luxury headphones and digital music players. These boxes were most likely empty as anyone accumulating enough tickets for them would have spent four to five times the actual value.

Behind the counter, leaning on his elbows reading a magazine was Leonard, as indicated by his nametag. He was in his early twenties, maybe twenty-five at the most, and could not have seemed less interested in his surroundings. I approached and slid the picture of Alana across the counter.

"You seen this girl hanging out here?" I asked, propping an elbow on the display case.

Leonard clearly saw the photo but took several full beats before he closed up his reading material and extended himself to full height. He took the picture of Alana in his fingertips and studied it, now looking from Cherry to myself and back again to Cherry, he said, "Who wants to know?"

I glanced at Cherry, indicating to her with my eyes that she take this one. People, especially young men, responded better to her than me. She quickly picked up what I was laying down.

"She is a, uh, an acquaintance of ours and we need to find her. We have reason to believe she might be in danger."

Interesting choice of words I thought to myself as Leonard raised an eyebrow of skepticism in Cherry's direction. He refocused his attention on the photo and I managed to shoot Cherry a *what was that* look.

"What if you're the danger?" Leonard said and placed the photo on the glass. "I wouldn't want to be party to something like that."

"Look kid, we just need to find this girl and ask her a few questions. We know she hangs out here. You seen her or not?"

Leonard refocused his attention on his magazine, flipping page by page very slowly. "Couldn't really say. Lots of kids come through here all day. Be hard to pick out one of hundreds," he said.

I saw where this was going. From my pocket I pulled a half fold of bills and ripped off two twenties, tossing them onto the counter. He snatched the money quickly, stuffing it into his faded blue jeans.

"She was here, I don't know, maybe half an hour ago with a

bunch of friends. Went out the side door alone, not five minutes before you showed up," he said.

"Which door?" Cherry asked.

Leonard shot a thumb toward a bright red EXIT sign hanging from the ceiling.

I knocked my knuckles on the glass, leaving a hollow echo behind. "Thanks," I said.

The lights in the parking lot sent a soft amber cast in small pockets under each lamppost. Cherry grabbed my elbow as we passed through one of these yellow-ish umbrellas of light and asked, "What's the end game here, Ellis? What if we had found her in there?"

I didn't want to say that I had no fucking clue but that was the truth. Usually in moments like those the first thing that popped into my brain was what came out of my mouth. That method worked at about a fifty-fifty clip and a few times damn near cost me my life. I started to get the feeling that this was turning into one of those situations. I knew I was never going to turn Alana over to the Kreski brothers, no matter what her transgression against them might be. She was a kid for fuck's sake and as corrupt as my morale code was I tried to stand for at least one or two things; kids and animals was the line I had drawn for myself although I would imagine that a certain German Shepherd guard dog would disagree with me.

"I haven't worked that out yet," I said. I moved away from her, briefly leaving her alone in the lemonade like halo. I could sense she wasn't following me and I turned and the shadow play on her hair and skin gave her an angelic look. She was a knockout but in that moment I thought I was seeing an illusion or a hopeful apparition of what I needed her to be for me. I retreated back to her. "What is it?"

"I just want you to keep your eyes on the prize. No more Kreskis, no more kids. Let's get this done and be done with it," she said.

"I got it," I said.

We found the Cutlass where we had left it, nestled in the shadows of the public lot. I slipped my key into the lock, swung the door open and sunk into the driver's seat. The moment I pulled the door shut I felt the cold cool steel of a gun against the base of my skull.

CHAPTER NINE

"DRIVE," THE SOFT FEMALE VOICE SAID. IT WAS almost a whisper.

"What about her?" I said, referencing Cherry, who had her hand on the passenger side door when she noticed the pistol pressed to my head. She was frozen in time.

"What about her?" she repeated. "You want to keep your head? Push the pedal and drive."

I did as I was told. Locking eyes with Cherry as the car pulled away. The fear was visible on her face.

The reflection from the rear view mirror displayed to me the soft, expressionless brown eyes from the photo crumpled in my back pocket. There was a glint that popped and faded from them as we passed underneath a lamppost. I maneuvered the Cutlass to the exit of the lot.

"Hello Alana," I said calmly.

The first blink from those eyes. Maybe she expected something else, more nervousness or calamity in my voice. This was not the first time I had a gun pointed at me nor against my head. She dug the muzzle of the weapon with added pressure into my skin.

"Just drive," she said.

"Where?" I asked.

"Broken Bow Point."

"The marshes? If you're going to kill me there are much better places. I can show you if you want?"

The frustration level was palpable from the backseat and for a fleeting second I thought she might plug me right there in the parking lot. The pressure loosened against my neck, the firearm briefly breaking contact.

"I'm not going to kill you. We're just going to talk."

"We have that in common, Alana. All I wanna do is talk to you so you think you could maybe take that thing off me? Pretty please?"

She hesitated then pulled the gun from my head. "Just drive. I don't care where."

That was the first time the words from her mouth sounded like the teenager she was. Every syllable to this point was hardened and chock full of confident attitude. Thinking about the group of girls from the arcade, I wondered how Alana fit their dynamic. Was she the alpha? Were the other girls frightened by her or envious of her brazenness? Maybe she was the aloof one of the group and her friends had no idea who she really was.

These thoughts cycled through my mind as I directed the car away from the lights of the boardwalk towards Atlantic Avenue.

We travelled in silence. The congestion out on the Avenue was light and I wasn't really sure where I was going. My eyes kept drifting to the rear view mirror and I was met with the same reflection every time. Alana watched me with no hint of an expression or tip of the cap to what she was thinking. I had plenty of thoughts running through my head. For one, where'd she get the gun? Although considering who her uncle was and where she lived it shouldn't have come as too much of a surprise. Was I being too naive in regards to Alana? Was her innocent face and pretty eyes and just a girl from the neighborhood looks blinding to me to what she might be? After all, I was holding a photograph of her delivered to me by some very nasty people who were not looking to have a play date with her. What had she done to run across these people? That's when it hit me. I knew exactly where to go.

It wasn't until we were ascending the ramp to merge onto the parkway that she spoke.

"Where we going?" she asked. Her voice didn't contain a drop of fear or anxiety, just plain curiosity, like asking a stranger for the time"

"I wanna show you something," I said.

She slumped back against the seat and her gaze drifted out the window. We headed south, passing under illuminated green exit signs attached to the many overpasses that crisscrossed over the highway. My grip tightened on the wheel. There was a chance I was making a deadly mistake. Approaching a situation head on and showing your hand can work if the atmosphere and players involved allow for it. But this girl was a wild card. I didn't see many options and what were the odds that I would get a one-on-one with her again? Like most things lately I just shrugged off my gut concerns and trudged on.

After about thirty minutes the landscape along the highway slowly started transitioned from an industrial, desolate look to an urban layout. In the distance the twinkling lights of the Victory City skyline shone brightly against the black, starless night. I liked to keep my distance from the city unless it was absolutely necessary. Too many big fish all trying to take bites out of each other. I preferred to keep to my own small-ish pond.

Well before the city center was upon us I took the Roosevelt Ave./Wyattville Exit. Along the main drag we passed an all night convenience store with a gas station attached to it, a sprawling brick apartment complex and several vacant mini-malls. We drove two miles from the highway before we entered a town center populated with a small courthouse overlooking a large square lawn with a tall statue of a forgotten man on a horse. From the center the road veered to the left and a stretch of shops and restaurants spread out in front of us. The street was lined with tall trees that matched the height of the two story structures on either side.

It was late by this point but the road was pock marked with cars parked along the sidewalk. I travelled to the end of the street where the frequency of restaurants began to thin out and whipped an illegal U-turn under a traffic light and started off back the way we came. A block and half up I managed to slide into an empty spot behind a large black Range Rover. I silenced the engine. I sensed Alana creep forward in her seat behind me. From my jeans I pulled the photo and offered it over my shoulder. She took it.

"What do you make of this?" I asked.

She was silent for a moment before replying, "My eighth grade photo. Where'd you get this?"

I pressed an index finger against the driver side window.

"There," I said.

Across the street and half a block up was an illuminated awning of bright blue and yellow advertising The Ukrainian Kitchen. The front window was large and light fell through it onto a set of tables for outdoor seating. Three large men loitered in front, smoking cigarettes and drinking from brown beer bottles. All of them wore bulky leather jackets with the same close-cropped crew cut. They could have been triplets from this distance.

"That place. That's where that photo came from," I said.

"The Kreskis," she said.

Now it was my turn to be caught off guard. That's happened a lot the last few days and it felt worse each time.

"How do you know these guys?" I asked.

"You first," she said.

This was one those times where you had to lay it all on the table, right? I adjusted the mirror to get a better look at Alana. Her focus was on the other side of the street.

"I contract for them. They send me targets and I find them," I said, swallowing hard, "and then I turn them over."

"That it?"

"More or less."

"That why you were down by me this morning? Cause you got this?" She flicked the edge of the photo, creating a popping sound as her finger slid off the edge.

"Yeah."

"What were you gonna do? Snatch me off the fucking street in broad daylight? Pretty dumb plan."

"I didn't know what I was doing. Listen Alana, you gotta tell me what you're into with these guys."

"Roman and Max. Animals. Both of them."

"Just give it to me straight. Maybe we can help each other out."

"Why should I trust you?"

"If you couldn't trust me your ass would be in there right now probably on a meat hook or some shit like that."

Her eyes locked on mine and it took a summoning of willpower to not look away. She was testing me, trying to peer inside me. I was right and I hoped that she knew it. She broke contact and looked out the window again. She was silent for a long time before:

"This big ass SUV jumps the curb and cuts me off on the sidewalk on my way home from school about two or three weeks ago. Shoves me in a car with two other guys and one of them, I think one of the brothers, I'm not sure, pulls out a gun and tells me that I'm gonna pick up a package and deliver it for them."

"What'd you say?"

"I told them to fuck off and spit on the one guy. Told them my uncle would cut their balls off when I tell him what they're doing."

The words came easy for her as if she was back in that car with the Ukrainians. She continued.

"They laughed at me. Then the big guy, Ruslan I think, says that my father was working for them when he got popped. Trafficking cocaine and they lost all this money because of him and now I have to do this to make up for his debt."

The men finished their smokes, flicked them into the street and retreated inside the restaurant. I felt the urge to go inside behind them and find Roman, attempt to talk it out. Alana would never be delivered into the Kreski's clutches if I had anything to do with it but with that realization came the reality that, in their eyes, my failure to bring her in would be a punishable offense. So now it was on me and there was no way to know how this one would play out. I thought about Cherry and what she would say. Probably something deriding before dropping some sage advice.

"What did your uncle say?" I asked.

Alana shook her head as she began to chew her bottom lip with her teeth. "Nah, not an option," she said. "They have men on the inside. Said they'd kill my father if I didn't do it. What else was I supposed to do?"

"So you took the package?" I said.

"Yeah but, I wigged out while I was walking, saw some cops and threw it into the canal. And I've been carrying this thing ever since," she said, waving the gun briefly in the air. A small pounding from a miniature hammer began behind my eyes and my back felt very tight. I rubbed my temples while simultaneously arching my back going into a deep full stretch. Fuck it.

"Stay here and keep your head down," I said.

Before she could respond I was out of the car and halfway across the street. I reached the sidewalk and tried hard not to think about what I was doing. I had never refused these guys and I had delivered every time so their reaction was a variable that I could not even pretend to predict. A large handle protruded from the metal framed glass door. I yanked it toward me and walked through the door.

CHAPTER TEN

ROMAN SAW ME FIRST. HE WAS SEATED AT A TABLE IN the far corner with two other men, sipping from small espresso cups and smoking thin black cigarettes. His face was a mixture of surprise, confusion and genuine happiness. In spite of what our relationship had evolved into there was a genuine respect that did exist between us.

The first time I saw Roman he was hitting the speed-bag at a dusty, rundown hard knock gym located off a back alley in the East Village. My trainer, Bobby Futch, had brought me there to spar with some of the local guys, see if I was ready to make a step up in class. Roman was small, a junior lightweight, but with lightning fast hands and a concrete chin. I was just an amateur then, like Roman, and we shared many nights when we fought on the same card. We bunked together, ate meals and travelled together. A time existed when I would have considered Roman one of my best friends but then the prizefights disappeared and we both went our separate ways into our post fight careers.

It was his brother Max who was the problem. Never skilled enough to get in the ring he inserted himself into Roman's career at every turn. The firing of trainers became routine and Max's antics cost Roman a promotional deal or two with some decent outfits. Max didn't like me and he knew how I felt about him. It always bothered me that Roman put up with all the bullshit that Max brought to the table but I had my own career to worry about at the time.

The Ukrainian Kitchen was nothing special visually. There were rows of tables with plastic flower print tablecloths with standard banquet hall chairs pushed underneath. The flooring was cheap linoleum and the walls were covered in faded green paint. I had only been here a few times and one detail always struck a chord of peculiarity; it never smelled like food. There was no aroma of ethnic delicacies simmering on a stovetop somewhere deep in the hidden kitchen. Not like Omar's place which hit your nose from three blocks away. I don't think food was on the menu here.

Roman rose to his feet and gestured me over to the table. Ruslan, a big gelatinous man, stood as well. I think he was a cousin or something. Roman told me the story once but I couldn't recall it. Max, with his back to me, remained seated. The two goons who were outside with Ruslan were nowhere to be seen.

"Pryvit...Priyvit" he said with a bright beaming smile across his face.

"Roman. Good to see you," I said.

We shook hands with a pull in close and clap on the back.

"Come, come, have a seat with us. Ruslan, get a chair," he said.

Ruslan pulled a chair from an adjacent table and slid it next to where Max was sitting.

I sat down in the chair and scooted in close so I could rest my elbows on the tabletop. "Hello Max," I said.

Max grunted, not necessarily in my direction but just in general. He kept his eyes on a newspaper splayed out in front of him. The dull gray pages had a large picture of a soccer player in mid kick. It was a foreign publication, Russian maybe.

Roman joined us at the table as Ruslan disappeared through a door behind us. "Ellis, my friend, drink?" he said.

I shot a finger toward one of the empty espresso cups on the table. "I could go for one of those," I said.

Roman yelled loudly to the back and a minute later Ruslan appeared with a silver pot and an empty porcelain cup. He placed them on the table in front of us and Roman did the honors.

It tasted like shit but I was far from a coffee snob. If it was brown and hot and remotely tasted like it was filtered through coffee grounds I would most likely drink it.

"So, what brings you here my friend? The girl?" he said.

"The girl?" I said, acting confused but fishing for Roman to tip his hand to his meaning.

"Yes, yes, the girl. Little bitch is tough. We knew she would not be so easy as the others. She likes to spit. Right, Max?" Roman laughed.

Max peeled his eyes from the newspaper. He did not share Roman's amusement.

"That's why I'm here, to talk about the girl." I said.

Roman reached into the liner of his jacket and pulled a fancy box of cigarettes from it. It was hard cardboard with gold leaf foiling on the sides. The markings were unfamiliar to me. Imported. The good stuff. He popped open the top, slid out a long black wrapped cigarette and took a lit match to it. He drug hard, the tip glowing an angry red as he did so and then blew out a violent stream of smoke from his lungs.

"So, let us talk then." Roman said.

"There have been some, let's say complications." I replied. There were several ways to handle these guys and most of them ended up bad. I was banking on my considerable leeway with the brothers considering my history with Roman and to a lesser extent, Max, who decided to pipe up.

"Complications? What complications?" he said.

"Explain," Roman said calmly, ashing his cigarette into an empty espresso cup.

"First, I wanna say to both of you that I appreciate what you guys have done for me the last couple of years. Who knows where I'd be, probably still parking cars or back in the ring with my brains turning to shit—"

"Get on with it," Max said through gritted teeth.

Roman raised a hand to calm his brother. He turned his attention to me before saying, "In our world, very difficult to find trustworthy individuals. It has been a pleasure my friend."

"She's just a kid, Roman. I told you once a long time ago, no kids. You want me to rough a guy up? Fine. Make some rounds on the money? All good. I'm your man. Pick someone up? I'm not a hundo on that but if the bread is right you know I'm in. Right?"

They both stared at me. Max tipped his chair back on two legs and stretched his arms behind his head, interlocking his fingers. A smile broke across his face revealing yellowed, jagged teeth. He said something to his brother in Ukrainian. Roman narrowed his eyes slightly.

"A kid you say? Yes?" Roman said.

Now it was Max's turn to laugh. A deep, baritone rumble that ignited in his belly and leapt from his throat. He brought his chair back down onto all four legs. He slapped his hand on the table as he rose and disappeared, mumbling in his language as he walked. Not understanding, I turned back to Roman and he was smiling also.

"Come with me. Come," he said.

He waved his hand as he rose from the table and disappeared through a brown swinging door against the back wall. I took two deep breaths, drained my now cold espresso and got to my feet.

I entered what I imagine was supposed to be the kitchen area. All the requisite equipment was in place. Gas range, flat top griddle and a large stainless steel prep table in the middle of the room were all where they were supposed to be. The air was free of grease or spice and the appliances looked brand new, shiny and twinkling as if fresh out of the box. I wasn't even sure they were plugged in.

On top of every available space there sat cases of shrink wrapped clear bottles. As I moved past the first case I could see it was a vodka with a bright blue label and yellow lettering in what looked like Russian but I couldn't be too sure.

Roman and Max were nowhere to be seen so when Ruslan came from behind a corner my first instinct was to jump backwards. He chuckled and shook his head at me.

"This way," he commanded.

Down a narrow dimly lit corridor I followed Ruslan until we made our way to the back of the building. The back door was open and the chill in the air swept in through a rusty screen door. To the left was another open door with stairs that disappeared below the floor. Ruslan pointed a meaty finger toward the stairs.

Awash in a soft blue glow from the overhead lights, the stairs were made of rotting wood that were most likely original to the structure. Each plank gave and splintered under my weight and I feared I would fall through them. I released the breath I had been holding when my feet touched the solid concrete floor at the bottom.

Across the room Roman stood at the opening of a large walk in freezer. The drop in temperature was noticeable even from where I was standing. He motioned with his hand and as my feet carried me across the room I suddenly began to sweat and become nervous. I could imagine that most people who ended up in the basement of The Ukrainian Kitchen weren't there to check the structural integrity of the stairs.

"In here, I want to show you your little girl," Roman said, now dead serious.

I maneuvered myself around the massive metal door to the freezer and stepped inside. Along the far wall were several tables with long black bags stretched out on each. Body bags. My heart stopped and my feet became implanted into the floor.

"Come here," Max said. He was in the corner unzipping one of these bags. Reluctantly I moved to him.

I instinctively closed my eyes as I arrived table side. The bag was open and I got a brief glimpse of the bluish skin, hard dried blood droplets and the lifeless pupils staring into oblivion before my own lids snapped shut. The circles I had found myself in throughout the course of my life had hardened me to these types of scenarios but there existed somewhere in my physiology things I could not control. Like the eyelids or the inability to manage my breathing in life threatening situations.

"Look," Max said, cupping a hand on the back of my neck and jerking it forward a few inches.

I opened my eyes and saw the small round holes caked in black blood, three of them, located in the chest, intermingled with matted black hair. His throat was open to the esophagus with white and maroon muscle matter frayed along the edges. The face was frozen in a state of anguish and struggle and the need to breathe. It was all there on his face.

Max released his stone like hand from my neck and my posture eased a bit. I turned my attention to Roman, who was leaning casually against the door jam.

"What's this?" I said.

He popped his body from the doorway and joined Max and I at the table.

"This was Vanya and he is in this state because of your supposed little girl," he said.

"You telling me she did this? Bullshit." I said, "She's a god damn child, Roman."

"You say is bullshit, eh? But what do you know of this?" he said, grabbing the end of the zipper and closing it above Vanya's contorted head.

"Vanya was good man. Strong man with wife and two children. And now he is this," he said, waving his hand toward the body.

"What happened?" I said.

"There was a meeting scheduled. Vanya was to drop off a

package to the girl and then return here. We found him dead in the backseat of his car."

"That doesn't sound too convincing, Roman."

Max cursed at me and spat on the floor. He turned and slammed his shoulder hard into my arm causing me to stumble backwards. I could put Max down pretty easily and he knew it. He also knew that I wouldn't do that here. Max exited the room and I could still hear the cursing from the outer room.

The whole thing was pretty weak in my mind but there was one question that fought its way to the front of my mind.

"Does the storing of corpses in the freezer adhere to the rules and regulations of the health code," I said. Uncomfortable humor. Another one of those things I couldn't seem to get handle on. "Seriously, Roman, what the fuck?"

"Serious business and you make jokes," he said, pulling another black cigarette from his pocket. "We were very fortunate to find Vanya before the authorities. Now he stays here until we can get him back to Kiev through less conventional means. But Vanya is no concern of yours. Your concern lies with the girl. She must be brought to me."

The tension was starting to build between us. I could see the muscles tightening around Roman's jaw bone. The cigarette smoke hung thick between us in the frigid air of the freezer. I decided to just lay it out for him.

"Roman, you have to understand that I can't bring that kid to you knowing what you'll do. Don't ask me to do that," I said.

"I've already asked you and now you refuse me," he said as he slowly backed away toward the door. He peered into the outer room before maneuvering the big metal door as close as he could to shutting it. He turned and approached me.

The cold became too much for me as my teeth began to chatter without my consent or control.

"Listen to me, my friend," he said, his frosty breath hanging between us before evaporating. "I care not for that man in the bag. Is actually quite a bit easier without him around. In a way, the girl did us a favor. But Max…is you know," he trailed off.

"I get it. What do you want me to do?"

Roman pulled the cigarette box from his pocket and offered the open box to me. I took one and slipped it between my lips with the hope that it would calm the involuntary spasms in my face.

"I will be in contact this week. Until then do nothing," he said as he cupped my elbow with his free hand and led me toward the door. "Come, I will walk you out."

Max was nowhere to be seen as we made our way back up the wooden stairs of death, through the kitchen and finally through the front door onto the sidewalk. The deep chill was still clinging to my skin as I lit up my cigarette with Roman's solid gold butane lighter.

I shot an inconspicuous glance toward the Cutlass but it was too far away to get a good look.

"Ellis, this business with the girl is bad for all of us. I need time. Let me walk you," he said.

A jab of panic hit me just above the stomach as I fell in line and we made our way diagonally across the street. My heart was starting to pound. A morbid curiosity overtook me as I became interested to see what exactly Roman's reaction would be if he saw Alana in my car, hunched down in the backseat, pistol in hand. Would she shoot it out with him right there on the street? Hard to tell but my curiosity ended as we got closer to the vehicle and I could clearly see that it was empty. No Alana. No gun.

I shook hands with Roman and told him I'd be waiting for his call which was bullshit but what else could I do at that moment.

As I headed back to Harbor Point I was trying to put the pieces together but I felt like I was running full speed down a steep hill without a plan to halt the tremendous momentum that had built up inside me.

CHAPTER ELEVEN

It was hot. Not so much in a sweltering temperature kind of way but the type of heat that generates when you've been laying in bed for three days. When I got home from my foray in Little Ukraine my first order of business was to call Cherry to give her the rundown and convince her I was alive and breathing. The concern in her voice and her willingness to come over almost broke me down but it was sleep that I needed.

Boris on the other hand had his own needs to worry about. What initially seemed like genuine feline concern for my well being quickly gave way to panicked hunger growls from behind his tiny fangs. If anyone happened to be standing outside my apartment they would have thought a cat was being tortured. He was a bastard sometimes. But he was mine and occasionally he managed to throw some attention my way, always on his terms of course, which was good enough for me. I shuffled my way through his feeding routine, taking the normal precautions not to step on the little fur ball as he weaved in and out between my legs and dodged my feet while I moved from the pantry to the counter. The ratio of wet to dry had to be precise or I would receive an expression that combined: "You can't be serious," with a dash of "Are you fucking mental?"

After nearly passing out from a head rush due to dropping Boris's bowl onto his mat and standing up too quick, I managed to stumble into the bedroom, strip off every layer of filthy, cigarette smoke infused clothing and hit the mattress. I think I was asleep before my aching head hit the pillow. A cliché for sure but true in this case. I think.

When I awoke, covered in a layer of sweat and drool, I felt better. The tiny man with a hammer behind my eyes had disappeared and a feeling of balance returned to my feet as I planted them on the floor and wiped the build up from my eyelids. An old brass clock on the dresser told me it was seven in the morning. Could that be right? I wondered what day it was. Boris's reaction was typical and as I stumbled to the bathroom I gave the little guy a perhaps harder than necessary nudge with my foot.

The hot water was cleansing. It crackled and awoke the pores in my skin, allowing it to breathe. After a complete scrub with some dollar store soap I emerged from the tub soaking wet. There was no towel hanging on the rack. Was that my doing or Cherry's? Probably mine.

I toweled down in the bedroom and then did a quick cleanup on the trail of water I had laid down from the bathroom.

A clean pair of jeans, a fresh pair of boxers and a soft T-shirt always made me feel a little better as I had a tendency to simply exist in what I was wearing for days on end. With my teeth brushed and the cat satisfied, I left by the back door without bothering to lock it. Fuck it.

Halfway down the iron staircase that led from my landing the hunger pains hit me. I had to get some food in my stomach.

No sign of the Ortiz clan as I slipped through the alley and out onto Filmore Street.

I strolled toward the ocean for about six block before I hit Jenni's. The bell did a dance above my head as I swung the glass door inward and approached the counter. It was a quaint little place. Six circular stools lined the Formica countertop that itself served as a dividing line between customer and kitchen. The flat top griddle nestled in the back corner smoked with an assortment of breakfast material. The phone rang off the hook and the large Bunn coffee machine was always percolating and the woman in the center of it all was Jenni.

"Where have you been hiding?" she said as she whirled around at the sound of the bell. In an earlier part of her life Jenni was most likely described as cute or mousey but at this point the crows feet and sun damage were beginning their assault on the adorable territory of her face. Still, she was lively and a good time. When I first started coming in here and was desperate for work I did deliveries for the corporate accounts she held. I'd do anything for her and she knew it but she never asked.

"Mornin', Jenni," I said.

"Usual?"

"Please."

I had been eyeing the cabinet of cigarettes since I walked in. I had extracted countless packs from the encasement and I wanted to do it again. Fuck it.

"And I'm gonna grab a pack of smokes," I said, over the sizzling meat.

"Since when?"

"Don't ask. It's been a rough week."

I grabbed a pack of Reds, packed them good against the palm of my hand, tore away the plastic and headed outside to indulge.

It was crisp and sunny in a way that those who knew could tell that summer was almost here. Several contractor trucks passed in front of me down Filmore; no doubt they were off to finish a summer rental for the throngs that would ultimately arrive in a few months. I usually did my best to avoid the center of Harbor Point during tourist season but the spillover rate into the outer neighborhoods had been rising the last few years.

The city itself was engaged in a cultural death match that had been raging on long before I got here. Many of the ethnic neighborhoods, whether it was the Puerto Ricans in The Pearl or the blacks in The Bottoms, were at risk when it came to prime time summer real estate and the image of the city. Cash money fueled the gentrification machine that pushed the eventual elimination of Little Beijing from the map to be replaced with the now under construction Harbor Point Outlets. Made me sick. One of the reasons I picked this place was that it wasn't a beach town. It was a city that happened to be on the water and it had some of that big city flair that I had been groomed on as a young man. Now, Harbor Point's fate would play out in boardrooms in City Hall, far from the grooves and pockets of reality that made this place special to me.

As thoughts of politicians and real estate robber barons thoroughly ruined the taste of my cigarette, a loud smoke billowing busted up blue Ford pickup turned the corner and rolled to a stop at the curb. The bed of the truck was over filled with netting, machine parts and garbage. A rotten smell crept into my nostrils.

Seeing the old bucket of rust made me chuckle. Partly because of the state of the vehicle itself and the sheer luck that must be involved to keep it on the road but mostly because the guy behind the wheel was genuinely one of my favorite people.

"Git over here you son of a bitch!" boomed a voice from the shadowy interior of the truck's cab.

I sprung myself from the wall and ambled over to the passenger side.

"How you been, Frank?" I said.

My elbow found a comfortable spot on the open passenger side window. Frank Manno, sometimes known as Butch to his friends, sat smiling from ear to ear. The four or so good teeth in his head sparkled against the deep red of his diseased gums. He was a large man, balding with gray stubble against his wrinkled skin. Frank must've been pushing sixty - sixty-five but you wouldn't know it.

"Ah, you know, a little of this, a little of that. Keeping the water freshly chummed," he said, behind a throaty laugh.

Two meanings could be gleaned from this. Butch ran a successful fishing operation in which he literally kept the waters full of bloody fish guts. There was of course the other thing. I decided to leave it there and toss a sideways smile back at him.

"What about you? Keeping that pretty face clean I see?" he said, referencing the trace bruising on my head from my run in with King Tito's boys. "I keep tellin' ya, you want some honest work with no risk of scraping the skin you come see me."

The idea of an honest day's work with Butch gave me no more a sense of security than venturing into the pseudo morgue at The Ukrainian Kitchen.

"You wanna go out?" he said.

It took me about two seconds to reply in the affirmative. I enjoyed the time on Butch's boat. Mainly for the calm of the ocean, being so far out to sea that you couldn't see the shoreline was a supremely enlightening experience but also for Butch's company. For all his brashness and penchants for vulgarity the old man never wanted anything from me. I could vent and not be judged out there on the water. In that moment I definitely needed a third party.

"Let me just grab my food," I said.

"Grab me a coffee, black. We got things that need discussin'."

My ass was numb after two blocks in the old jalopy. Trying to eat a greasy breakfast sandwich and balance a steaming paper cup of coffee between my legs became a struggle I was quickly losing. Butch slurped his coffee, not well, as a small coffee stain rapidly began to grow on his shirt.

"You seen her yet?" he said, as he gunned the gas to make it through a yellow traffic light.

"Seen who yet?" I said, already knowing.

"Don't play dumb with me boy. I spied her down at the boat yard a week, week and half ago. Marty had some parts from a junker that came in and while I was there I saw her with some woman going into the office. Knew sooner or later she'd end up on your doorstep. Like a puppy dog. With rabies. Probably fleas, too."

His no judgment zone didn't extend to Cherry.

It didn't do any good to lie to the man when he already knew the truth. I jammed the last of the sandwich into my mouth and clutched the coffee in my hands to stop the burning on the inner parts of my thighs.

"Yeah I saw her. She came by my place."

Butch let out a grunt as he navigated the truck onto Atlantic

Avenue. There were large signs of varying colors directing traffic to the various districts in the city. From here if you wanted the Casino you stayed in the left lane, the boardwalk and the Atlantic Circle you hung to the right. We stayed dead center and followed the big blue sign for the Harbor Point Marina District.

The rest of the short trip we took in silence. As the road dipped down toward the water the raised and bobbing sails crept into view. The marina wasn't huge but there were a number of pleasure boats docked to one side with the commercial tour boats on the other end of the long wooden dock. I heard somewhere there was an expansion plan in place.

Butch navigated the smoke monster into a private lot for owners across the street and promptly hit a garbage can, spilling the contents across the pavement, before jamming the gear into park. I was lucky to be alive.

"C'mon, I need help with some stuff in the back."

Butch lowered the rusty tailgate. The bed of the truck was a mini junkyard filled with an assortment of, well, junk. He grabbed two large jugs of red liquid and motioned to a medium sized leather satchel. It had seen better days. I threw the heavier than expected bag over my shoulder, closed the tailgate and caught up to Butch who had already started off across the lot.

The only thing I knew about boats is that I liked them. Liked the way they looked, liked riding on them, liked jumping off them. The time investment to learn the necessary skills to pilot one did not interest me. That's what guys like Butch were for.

The vessel was named the *Never Say Never* and it wasn't the biggest or the fanciest thing in the water but it got the job done for me as well as Butch's business. Roomy enough for larger groups but not too big so that a smaller group wouldn't feel worth the effort.

I dropped the leather satchel on the deck and made my way to the front of the boat, my usual spot. As I sipped my coffee I watched Butch amble around the boat, readying it for launch. He was a very strange man but over the years I had come to understand that he wasn't everything he gave to most people. There was that wiseguy from Buffalo who hinted at what kind of guy Butch was in a previous life. Butch himself was not forthcoming with that kind of information but from what I had pieced together there was a dangerous streak to this toothless teddy bear. A high profile skimming operation, prison time, a riot during said prison time and even a bank robbery while he was AWOL from the Navy. Nothing confirmed nor denied but speculated nonetheless.

"You ready, cupcake?" he shouted.

I threw back a thumbs up. The engine roared to life and we crept slowly out to sea and the distant horizon line.

It was about twenty minutes of travel and I was in full trance mode. Never got into meditation or anything new-agey but this was as close to peace of mind that I could get.

The low hum and rumble of the engine cut out and the *Never Say Never* hung in the water, bobbing up and down, carrying my body in the sway. Butch emerged from the back with the leather satchel slung over his shoulder and joined me at the front. An unlit cigarette dangled from his mouth as he dropped the bag next to me. I fished a lighter from my pocket and extended my arm, offering it.

"No, trying to quit," he said.

"How's that going for you?" I said

"It's a process," he said, rolling the cigarette back and forth between his wet lips.

Butch grabbed the zipper on the satchel and yanked. It

yielded begrudgingly through the rusted seams. He plunged a meaty claw inside and came up with a black revolver with the grip wrapped in duct tape. He nonchalantly tossed it over board. One after another this played out until eight pieces went over the side. He shrugged his shoulders at me.

"Waste management," he laughed.

There were certain things all of us did to live life the best way we knew how. For both of us that involved skating on the other side of the law. I decided in that moment that Butch was someone I would want in my foxhole.

"I'm working on something. You interested?" I said.

"Always interested. Until I hear the hair-brained ideas behind the something," he said.

I lit a cigarette and flipped ashes over the side. He eyed me up, watching the smoke escape from my lips. I was about to open my mouth and lay it out for him but he cut me off.

"Don't say what you're about to say if it involves what's her name. What's her name again?"

"Cherry"

"Don't bother. For that I ain't interested."

I never could quite nail down the precise situation that caused Butch's animosity toward Cherry but he never held it back when it came to her that's for sure. It was a long shot but I decided to press ahead anyway.

"Life changing money. That's all I'll say."

"Gotta better chance of catching Moby Dick with a fishing rod. Shit don't exist kid. It's a dick rip."

"What if it did exist though?"

"The guys who wear the fancy suits up on Plantation Hill, the guys who carry golf clubs instead of those pieces I just dumped. Those are the only stiffs that can steal money like that and get away with it. Guys like you and me? We get the bracelets. And your little philly? One way ticket to bracelet city."

"You know something I should?"

"Yeah, I know how to trust my gut when it's yellin' at me."

"Okay, okay. I had to ask."

"Appreciate the offer. Now give me that fucking lighter."

"What happened to the process?"

"Fuck it."

We smoked in silence, letting the breeze and soft spray cover us. After extinguishing his butt over the side, Butch checked his watch and headed to the back of the boat. The engine roared to life and we began a steady loop around back toward the marina.

Maybe Butch was right. I didn't want to push the Cherry issue too hard, partly out of fear of what he might say but either way I had a decision to make. In or out. I wanted to be champion of the world at one point in my life and took a lot of needless and reckless risks to try and get there. It never panned out for me but I got damn close and as I rode back to shore, I felt like that again. You only get a few chances to wear the crown. Who cares if second prize is a set of bracelets.

Fuck it.

"Ellis, get your ass back here," Butch snapped from behind the steering wheel.

My eyes snapped open. In that moment of clarity I must have dozed off. I pried myself from the cushion and managed to keep my balance under control, making my way to the captain's station.

"What's up?" I said.

"There," he said.

We were at a crawl now, moving through the marina. Butch pointed to the spot where the *Never Say Never* called home. A figure was standing on the dock. At this distance he was fuzzy and out of focus. I squinted hard and it became quite clear who it was, patiently waiting, hands clasped behind his back.

The Newspaper Man.

CHAPTER TWELVE

I stepped onto the dock as Butch began the routine of tying the boat to the wooden posts stationed at the front and the back. I could feel his eyes on me as I approached the Newspaper Man.

He was an odd looking man. Thick, large black rimmed glasses rested upon an even larger nose. On the two occasions I saw him I thought he was balding but now close-up it was clear his head was free of any hair follicles, his wrinkled face as well. He wore a simple storm gray tweed suit. If I had to guess he was in his sixties.

His hands were still clasped behind his back and he rocked back and forth on his heels slightly as I got closer to him. A half smile creased his face.

He spoke first.

"Mr. Boone, there are pressing matters that need your attention. If you would please accompany me to my office all will be explained," he said.

His voice was soft but not old man soft or grandfatherly in

any way. It was deliberate and measured with a slight accent slipping in with each syllable. Eastern European maybe.

"Who are you?" I said.

"Again, Mr. Boone, if you would please accompany me to my office all your questions will be answered," he said.

He unclasped his hands and swung his right arm wide, drawing my attention to a black town car, parked along the curb above the dock. His hand was missing two fingers and covered in smooth red and white scar tissue.

Butch came up behind me and dropped his claw on my shoulder.

"Just say the word, Boone, and Mr. Magoo here goes in the drink," he said.

No reaction from the Newspaper Man. Not a blink of an eye or flinch in his posture.

"It's okay, Butch, I think I can handle it," I said.

"That I am positive of, my friend. Come by this week. Do some fishing," he said.

Butch passed the small European man with a toothy snarl. Again, no reaction except for a dismissive side eye. His body remained completely still and stiff yet I got a sense of impatience in him. Almost as if he could think of anywhere else he'd rather be than here.

"Listen pal, you gotta understand that I can't get into that car with you unless I get a little more," I said.

"If you insist but I assure all will be answered. Time is of the essence, Mr. Boone," he said.

He adjusted his glasses and flexed his jaw. He was an odd creature I thought as he went through a little routine before speaking again. Realizing I was not going to break he relented.

"My name is Savić and I represent a man who is very eager to speak with you. Now you know who I am. Will you accompany me to my office?" he said.

I could have refused flat out but I needed to see what he, or his client had to say. If I was going to give myself over to Cherry's plan, however crazy and illogical it may be, I had resigned myself to take a shot at the chip if it was there and this man was somehow connected. Savić was a piece of the puzzle and in that moment I thought it was in my best interest to see where he fit.

"Lead the way," I said.

He turned quickly, a hunch to his posture and slight limp was present in his walk. He moved quickly up the incline toward the waiting car. I had to hurry to catch up.

I expected a driver but Savić slid behind the wheel and brought the engine to life, giving it a little too much gas. I thought he might pull away without me and when I reached for the handle to the rear passenger side door it was locked. Savić was fumbling by the window trying to find the right button to unlock the doors. After a moment the door clicked and I was able to get in.

It was a typical transportation car, used by every airport car service in the area: tinted windows and leather seats. An illusion of luxury. We moved at a brisk pace as Savić navigated side streets and service roads. He took a corner or two very tight and rubbed the curb with the rear tires causing me to slide across the slick interior of the backseat. It wouldn't have surprised me to find out this man did not have a driver's license.

We sped across Atlantic Avenue, practically running a red light. It appeared as if we were headed toward Altamont Square, the geographical center of Harbor Point. Named after a military hero long forgotten, the Square or more appropriately several squares, housed the city's administration hub. The courthouse, police department and City Hall all lined a meticulously manicured garden square with a towering statue of the aforementioned Altamont, a raised saber clutched in his stone fist. Just beyond the square proper were several other township buildings as well as commercial properties that housed Harbor Point's business district.

One building, a mini high rise called the Meridian Tower was a particular eye sore to the surrounding beauty of the area. A hulking monolith of office space stacked up floor by floor, the Tower was meant to represent the city's economic resurgence but a series of shady development deals delayed the completion and sent many prospective tenants fleeing for more stable environments.

Savić weaved us around the square, past the courthouse and down Centennial straight for the Meridian. Another curb was hopped as the car dove down into the depths of the underground parking garage. The tires squealed slightly against the slick road surface until we came to a spot next to an elevator entrance. There were only a handful of other vehicles in sight.

The engine was off and Savić was out of the car before I could get my fingers around the handle. His shoes echoed loudly against the gigantic emptiness of the garage. By the time I reached the elevator, he was holding it open with his three fingered hand to prevent it from closing. What was the rush? The door closed and we slowly rose up through the guts of the Meridian Tower.

The two of us were in close quarters now. He kept his eyes straight ahead watching the digital numbers above the elevator door rise and rise. He smelled like cheap cologne and cigars, very musty and generally unpleasant. Our upward ascent slowed and came to stop on the twentieth floor and with a soft ding of an invisible bell. Savić was on the move again, taking long purposeful strides with his gimpy leg until we came to a door with no sign or nameplates. No indication of a business or practice of any kind. The whole floor seemed devoid of any activity and for the first time I felt a sting of nervousness.

The old man unlocked the door and pushed it inwards and I followed him into an empty room, save for a small desk and two basic chairs. I was relieved to see that there wasn't plastic lining the floor and I relaxed a little. Savić was at the desk. He pulled off his jacket and draped it around one of the chairs. He checked his watch and with his other hand motioned for me to sit in the chair opposite him.

"Sit. It is almost time," he said.

I took a seat in a hard wooden chair while Savić fumbled through a drawer across from me. On the desktop he placed a medium sized electronic tablet, its screen fading in and out of various nature landscapes. He sat and leaned back in his chair, staring at me with a empty look.

"What now?" I said, completely confused.

"We wait," he said.

For a solid six minutes we sat in silence. My attempts at extracting information from Savić proved unsuccessful and nothing was given away in his demeanor nor his facial expressions.

Growing up with no money and parents who worked themselves harder than they should have forces kids to use their imagination and come up with a laundry list of stupid games and competitions. This is what my brother and I excelled at. Staying up late, waiting for our mother to come home, we would engage in epic staring contests over and over again. I was victorious most of the time, mostly because I was older than Darryl and he was an easily distracted child. But now I was in the Thunderdome of dry eyes and stiff lids. Savić was a pro, giving nothing and appearing as if he might have left his body for another time and place.

An obnoxious vibration broke the one sided competition as the tablet's screen came to life with a large green icon in the shape of a phone. Above the icon the words "Incoming Call" were displayed in white text.

"I believe you have a phone call, Mr. Boone," Savić said.

My forefinger tapped the icon transforming the screen into a video chat. In the lower right corner I could see myself and exactly where the camera on the tablet was framing me. The remaining screen real estate was dedicated to a thin, wiry man in a bright orange jump suit. His head was shaved except for a close cut goatee. He was looking off camera as the screen began to shake.

"Just fucking hold it steady," the man said.

His eyes refocused on the screen and we were looking directly at one another.

"I don't have a lot of time here so I'm just gonna fucking cut to it. I know everything, okay, everything you've been doing, everybody you've been hanging out with. The trip up north with that little black bitch. I get it all, I see it all. So here's my piece to you. Leave that office, go back to your little shitbox and your fucking bean burritos and walk away from this because it doesn't end well for you or that bitch or my stupid fucking wife," he said.

Andrew Kramer. Cherry said he fancied himself a gangster and it certainly seemed that way. He delivered his threat in a calm and cool manner, almost a whisper.

"I think you got the wrong guy."

"The fuck I do," he said, moving closer to the screen, "listen to me very carefully. That money is mine and mine alone. I'll be out of this fucking hell-hole soon enough and if you continue down the road you're on you are dead man. You hear me? With one phone call, lights out. Shit, I give the word and Savić makes you go boom."

He was very agitated now. The screen began to dip and cut part of his head from the screen.

"Hold the fucking thing still for Christ's sake! Don't make me say it again. I swear to God," he screamed at the unseen cameraman.

I wondered if he would make the type of threats he was tossing around if I was in that room with him, presumably his cell. Maybe he would think twice. Maybe he wouldn't but then we could settle our matter in a way I was more comfortable with.

The image righted itself and was held steady once again. I honestly didn't know how to react. Shrug my shoulders? Get up and storm out? Go across the desk and turn the two bit elderly European hit man's face to sawdust? I could easily show Kramer who he was dealing with and make him understand on terms he might comprehend.

"I understand," I said.

"Good. That's it. I'm done talking to you," he said. Kramer leaned in and the screen went black. I placed the tablet back upon the desk. Savić was out of his chair stuffing his arms into his jacket.

"Now that you realize and see the scope of the environment you are playing in you can better understand the utter insignificance of your existence," he said.

My ass was out of the seat and I had Savić up against the wall before he could blink. I pressed my forearm under his chin and hard against his throat.

"What is this? Think you can just pick me up off the street and threaten me? " I growled. This tactic was preferable to me than arguing with someone I couldn't get to. Kramer was a non-issue for me at the moment. Savić on the other hand was right there and available to see if he would spill anything.

"You have failed to see the danger you have placed yourself in," he managed to rasp out between pursed lips and gritted teeth. His wind was failing him. "I suggest you let me go."

I stepped back and watched as Savić regained his breath and composure. Once the air returned to his lungs, he straightened his wrinkled shirt and finished putting on his jacket. "You are in more danger than you realize, Mr. Boone."

CHAPTER THIRTEEN

I pulled into the lot of Steelhaven Mortuary Services and found a spot around the side of the large white stone building. It was late afternoon and the sun was beginning its descent toward the horizon. There were two other cars and a landscaping van in the lot. One I recognized as Cherry's.

It was a risk coming here so soon after the meeting with Savić and Kramer. After leaving the Meridian Tower I walked back to my apartment to fetch my car and planned on driving to the funeral home straightaway. Instead I meandered around Harbor Point, filling up the tank and driving aimlessly, my mind pouring over the events of the morning. I should have had Butch drop Savić in the water.

The direct threats weren't the problem, for me at least. I was mostly concerned about Cherry. I have had a tendency in my life to move toward danger instead of away from the hostilities. Maybe it was due to spite and stubbornness but after the run in with Savić I wanted to show them I wasn't afraid of their words. No doubt there was some goon or goons watching me as I sat in my car. Perhaps it was Savić himself. Just being here was a middle finger to them, whoever they were.

I exited the car and lit a cigarette. The gravel stone crunched under my feet as I made my way around the back of the building. The pathway sloped down and led to a smaller, separate parking lot with two hearses, both shiny black, backed up to a couple of bay doors. This small lot had a separate access road that disappeared into the woods that ran along the back of the property.

I made my way back around front when from across the lot, a small-ish middle aged man whistled and made his way toward me. When he got close he wasn't as small as I had originally thought. He was about my height, slicked back black hair and a thick bushy mustache. His brown shirt had a logo on the left breast that read Mario's Master Cuts, Lawn and Landscapes.

He pointed at my burning cigarette and said, "You think I could bum one of them from you?"

I dug out another smoke and the lighter and handed him both. He jabbed the cigarette into his mouth, struck the lighter and placed the flame to the tobacco and inhaled deeply. His eyes shut as he held the smoke in his lungs for a long while before releasing a stream of gray smoke through his nostrils.

"Enjoying that?" I said.

"It's been over five years since I've had one of these," he said.

"Seems to be going around."

"What?"

"Nothin', what's got you smoking again?"

"Just lost the contract on this place."

My eyes swept the surrounding grounds. Everything was lush and meticulous. Beautiful some might say.

"Not for the quality of work I hope," I said.

He let out a soft chuckle, "No. The way it was explained to me was that the business has been sold off and anything having to do with the new owners will have to be renegotiated. The owner said she'd pass on a recommendation for me but I ain't too hopeful."

"Sold? To who?" I said.

"Beats me. Probably one of those big corporate joints. Was a time when I had all the funeral homes in the area. Now most of them are owned by the Salem Company just with different window dressings," he said.

"The illusion of choice."

"Amen. This outfit has their own vendors they work with so I never once got back a contract I was axed from."

"Did the owner say why she is selling. Business not doing so hot?"

"The death business is the best business."

He flicked the cigarette into a bush, the lingering smoke creeping through the green shrubbery. He smiled at me before he said, "Hey, not my problem anymore. Thanks for the smoke. Now I gotta go break the news to my wife."

He turned and made his way to a white van parked in the corner of the lot. I watched as he started the engine and pulled the van to the exit. He waved as he maneuvered out onto the main road. I waved back.

I stepped inside into a large open space with a sitting area to the left and a large fish tank lining the wall to the right. White marble floors stretched throughout the entrance area. The sitting room contained a few couches, an old Egyptian rug and a fireplace that didn't appear to be functional. It was drab and out of place among the marble floors and the gold and crystal chandelier that hung from the ceiling. A hold over from a previous era perhaps. The fish tank, on the other hand was vibrant and alive with several different kinds of tropical fish that darted through the water, navigating a large shipwreck scene that sat above fluorescent blue stones.

I moved to the glass and watched two playful fish engage in a game of hide and seek amongst the various obstacles of the tank. I got so caught up that I didn't hear the clacking of heels on the marble floor that approached behind me.

"What are you doing here, Ellis?" Cherry said. She had an annoyed look splashed across her face.

I turned to face a woman who over the last couple of days didn't conjure the rage in my belly as she used to. She looked great, as always, even with her head cocked to the side and her hand on her hip, indicating her frustration level with me at the moment.

"Hey! Just thought I'd pop in to see where you worked. See how things are going," I said. I did it with a big smile and a hands up peace offering. I knew I should've called before surprising her like this. Cherry hated surprises in all forms.

She raised an eyebrow before she said, "Not cool. You shouldn't be here and anything we need to discuss can be done, you know, not here. You need to go."

"You're right. Shoulda called. Got it. But we should move now. Get a team together and get going. There have been some interesting developments that I wasn't comfortable sharing over the phone."

"What kind of developments?"

A new set of heels clacking against the marble floor now

approached us. Cherry grabbed my arm and looked me dead in the eyes. "Just play along, okay?" she said.

Cathy Meyer turned the corner and made her way to the fish tank. She looked to Cherry first before turning her attention to me. She said nothing as she studied my face. I got a weird feeling immediately and felt out of sorts in her intense stare. She was a tall woman, with shoulder length bright yellow hair, dressed in a plain gray jacket and matching skirt with a white blouse. Aside from her piercing eyes everything about her was plain. I turned away from her stare to look at Cherry and I instantly could not recall her face until I saw it again.

"This is, uh, John Smith and he, uh, wanted to see about some of our cremation services," Cherry said, breaking the awkward silence among the three of us.

"Ah, yes, cremation. Yes," she said. There was a slight hint of an English accent in her voice. "Cherry darling, grab the new client forms and meet us in the conference room," she said as she turned and started off down a long corridor that ran away from the front entrance. "This way, Mr. Smith," she shouted as she got further away."

I looked at Cherry and mouthed the words, "Mr. Smith?" She threw up her hands in exasperation and shoved me the direction of the hallway.

"Now Mr. Smith, what can we help you with today?" Cathy said as we sat across from each other at a large table. I had followed the sound of her echoing heels down the long hallway and through a half opened door into a conference room. It had the oak table in the middle of the room and was surrounded with several chairs but that was it.

I was stumbling my way through a response when Cherry came in and picked up the slack. "Mr. Smith was looking for a simple cremation and ceremonial urn for display," she said. Cherry passed a clipboard with a form attached to Cathy.

We spent the next ten minutes or so filling out a form with fake information where I concocted a parent on death's door who would be kicking off at moment. The explanation was that I wanted to be prepared and have everything ready.

"I just don't how much time we have but I think it would be best to have a plan in place so when the time comes we can move at a moment's notice," I said, while shooting a side-eye at Cherry. Cathy fiddled with the forms. I was trying to send Cherry an indirect message but she gave me no indication that she was picking up what I was laying down this time.

"It is all very simple in the end. With no burial service we will provide pick up from the place of death, be it at the hospital or at home and transfer the remains to our facility here where transport to the crematorium will be scheduled and executed. Upon receipt of full payment you can then pick up your loved one here at your earliest convenience," she said.

"Sounds like a well oiled machine," I said.

"It is," she said, annoyed. "Would you like to see our showroom? We have many urns available here on site and others that can be ordered. I will get the brochure from my office. Cherry, please show Mr. Smith into the showroom."

Cathy took the paperwork and exited the room.

"She seems pleasant," I said.

"Shut up," Cherry said as she rose from her chair and led me out of the room, down yet another hallway and into a big room lined with all the offerings to prospective clients.

Caskets in shiny mahogany and sleek gunmetal gray were situated to one side of the room while the urns were on the other. The options seemed like overkill but everyone has their own personal style even in death. My style consisted of pure nonchalance. Toss my ashes in the garbage for all I care. Cherry led me to a corner that had some urns lined up on several shelves.

"If I'm gonna be in we need to go as soon as possible. Are you ready? You know where it is?" I said in a whisper.

"Yeah I got it. Nailed it down a couple of days ago. What's the rush all of a sudden? And what developments were you talking about? What's going on?"

"I'll explain later. Can you come by tonight and we can go over all this shit. I have an idea on how to get it out of the ground clean."

"Fine. I'll be by later. You pick up the food."

Cathy entered the showroom holding a large brochure in her hand. She weaved her way through the rows until she found Cherry and I in the corner.

"Here is all the information you will need on our services. Once you are ready we can finalize everything and begin the execution of final wishes," she said.

She extended her hand and I took it. It was a very firm but delicate handshake. I imagined if birds had hands this might be what if felt like to shake hands with one.

Once again, Cathy studied my face as her hand was in mine. "Ms. Daniels, please see Mr. Smith out when he is finished here. I have several phone calls to make," she said. And like that she was gone. She was a very strange woman.

"What's up with her man?" I said.

"C'mon fool, let's go," Cherry said. She grabbed my arm just above the elbow and led me out of the showroom, past the conference room and back to the fish tank.

I shot Cherry a wink of my eye as I slipped through the front door and back out into the parking lot. She just stared at me.

I turned the car on and sat idling in the lot. It was probably a mistake to show my face here especially if I was going to be digging up a grave across the street in the coming days or weeks. But the impending sale complicated things a bit and not a mention of it by either Cherry or Cathy Meyer. Between the plan to actually get the coffin out of the ground, to my run in with Savić, to the strange bird Meyer; Cherry and I had a lot to discuss over dinner.

As I backed my car out of the lot there was a slight rustling from one of the windows. The white curtain that filled the frame swayed back and forth, unnoticeable except I happened to be looking right at it. I directed my car toward the exit but kept my eye on the window in my rearview mirror. Right before I pulled out onto the main road I could see Cathy Meyer, a scowl scrawled across her face, staring at me from the window.

CHAPTER FOURTEEN

LO'S WAS A PLACE THAT I DISCOVERED ON A JOB. I WAS tracking a Chinese émigré turned diamond smuggler and one of his frequent hangouts was this small dingy takeout place tucked between the marina and the casino district. The place itself, and its proprietor Lo, were not involved in any of the nefarious dealings of my target but if you wanted an authentic Chinese meal then his was the spot. After trying the food once there isn't a better place to hit in Harbor Point.

There were only a few tables in the small, rectangular restaurant so takeout was usually the only option or you'd be waiting a decent stretch to get a seat. I sat on a rickety plastic chair against the wall waiting for my order to be called. It gave me some time to mull over the events of the day although it was hard amongst the intoxicating aroma of fried rice, grilled meat, and the loud clanging of pans and occasional shouts in Chinese.

That the money had to come out of the ground was no question to me any longer and I had a pretty good idea how to get it done. The number of people we would need and who they would be was another question. I was almost certain that

Cherry would object to at least one of my proposed members. Then came the thought of how to deal with Savić and Kramer and how serious a threat they were. Cherry had mentioned that Kramer had maybe been dealing with the Celestials and that would be another problem. Those bikers, who had their headquarters out on the Slatsville Pike, made the Hell's Angels and Pagans look like toddlers or cute baby kittens. Toddlers holding cute baby kittens.

My order number was called and I rose and walked to the counter. It was decided. After dinner I'd lay it all out for Cherry and see her reactions and where the connections fell. It would have to piece itself together as we put the plan into action.

Lo's wife Zhen was at the cash register beaming at me. It had been a few months since I had been here. She was a small woman with short dark hair and soft eyes. Her smock was pock marked with stains from the kitchen. She worked as hard as anyone at the restaurant. In stark contrast to her husband her English was remarkable, with only a slight accent invading her speech.

"Hello, Ellis! Where have you been? My food no good for you anymore? Where's the new place? I burn it down," she said, laughing deeply as she rung up my order on an old manual cash register.

"Never. You know this is my place. I wouldn't cheat on you guys like that," I said.

"Good, good. Be careful with all those tacos you eat. Too much sour cream make you fat!" she said.

I handed her cash for the food and picked up a plastic bag containing a box of chicken chow fen, two servings of oxtail soup and a bucket of fried rice with some egg rolls for good measure. After a few good deeds done in the past they had refused to take payment from me anytime I came in to eat but we have come to an understanding over the years; I pay for my food at Lo's now. I've survived well in Harbor Point on the barter system. Help a guy out with a problem and occasionally you get a free combo platter but I was uncomfortable with those freebies extending forever. And they understood.

I blew her a kiss and told her to keep the change. Before I stepped away from the counter she waved me in close.

"My husband need to speak with you, not urgent he says but he will come and find you when time is right. He has something that will interest you very much he say," she whispered from across the counter.

"I'm not a hard man to find. He knows where I am. Tell him whatever he has I'll take a look at it," I said.

With my food in hand I stepped out onto the rain slicked street. I couldn't wait. As I walked the two blocks to my car I dug into the bag and shoved an egg roll into my mouth, ripping the fried dough in half with my teeth. The entire roll was gone before I started the ignition on the Cutlass and pulled out, headed for home.

The alley outside my apartment was dark when I cut the lights and killed the motor. That damn streetlight at the entrance was always blowing out. It had started to drizzle again and the raindrops filled the glass windshield. I hated the rain.

I got out, slammed the door and went to the trunk to fetch a windbreaker I had stored in a travel bag. Maybe I would need it for later. Trying to balance the bag of food in one hand and root around the crowded trunk with the other proved more difficult than I anticipated. The leather duffle was under a set of jumper cables and after extracting the windbreaker I tossed the bag to the back, unzippered. I'd get to it later. With the jacket slung over my shoulder I shut the trunk. That's when I saw them. Two large, shadowy figures moving slowly toward me. The gravel crunched lightly under their feet.

Breath escaped through my mouth and nostrils as I exhaled deep and hard. This wasn't what I wanted to be doing. It never was but that was part of it. There was always someone out there looking to get back at you or get you before you came for them. It was becoming harder and harder to keep track of everyone so at some point I stopped caring and dealt with the goons on a first come, first served basis.

My fist tightened on instinct alone. I placed the jacket and food on the slick trunk and readied myself. These guys were gonna pay a little extra for making me wet and possibly having to eat cold Lo's. At the front of the car they separated, each taking a side. I couldn't make out their faces but they were big boys at the least. They had to angle themselves to fit between the car and the brick wall in the alley. When they reached the doors I back peddled a bit to give myself some room to work and that's when I felt it. The hard metal against the back of my head. I froze instantly and put my hands up as the barrel of the gun pressed into my skull hard. I was brash but even I realized and respected the power of the firearm. This wasn't the movies.

My feet carried me forward into the arms of one of the approaching henchmen. Now I got a good look at his face. It was Rulsan, one of the Ukrainians from The Kitchen. I knew now who held the gun and as I was thrown against the brick wall I saw Max's face, smiling a crooked toothed grin. He came at me and jabbed the gun into my cheekbone. It glinted in the moonlight and my eyes moved from the barrel to Max's face.

"Pig fuck," he said in guttural broken English.

His breath smelled of cheap vodka and cigarettes. There was nowhere for me to go and my brain was searching for a way out of this but that gun made it difficult for the synapses to fire. Max glared at me before loading up his mouth and spitting directly into my face. It was hot and wet and began to mix with the rainfall as it oozed down my nose and onto my lips.

"Big tough guy, yes? Not so tough now, huh?" he said.

"What do you want, Max? You think Roman is gonna be happy when he hears this shit?" I said.

He removed the gun from my cheek and took a step back but he was still too close for my comfort. He laughed and looked back at the two giant Ukrainians, who were also laughing.

"Roman? Roman have nothing to say about what Max does, ever," he said and he laughed again deeply.

My mind flashed forward to some coup Max had pulled off with Roman as the one zipped up in one of those black body bags in the basement. Would Max really do that to his own brother? Part of me answered in the affirmative and then genuine fear ripped through me.

"What is this then? You gonna gun me down right here?" I asked.

"No, no, no. There will plenty time for you and this," he said, shaking the weapon at me. "Now is business time. The little bitch killer. You bring her to me. No shit, no excuses. Twenty-four hours or I be back and then, no talking. You see how easy for me to get you, yeah?" he said.

"I already told Roman I'm out on the girl. No kids," I said. After hearing Max's words I relaxed a little knowing he wasn't just going to shoot me here in the alley. He still thought he needed me so I said, "Go get her yourself. You know where she is."

There was hesitation in Max's response when he said, "No, must be you. You bring her to me and maybe I not kill you. Maybe," he said. Then I knew why he was outsourcing this job.

"You don't want King Tito clapping back. Is that it? You're afraid of going to war with the Puerto Ricans? I'm disappointed in you, Max."

One of the giant Ukrainians stepped around Max and landed a crushing blow to my rib cage, the sound of cracking bone echoed in the alleyway. I doubled over and struggled to catch my breath. I had broken a few ribs during my time in the ring and it was worse every time it happened. The pain surged up my side and into my armpit. I was lifted to my feet by my assailant. Max stepped forward and put his hand around my throat.

"If I not have girl in twenty four hours this will feel like holiday to you. Yes?" he said.

Another fist, this time to my midsection, eliminated any air that I had managed to suck into my body. I wheezed and coughed without control.

"Time running out on you, Boone," Max said as he raised the gun high above his head. The reflection caught my eye and I looked as he brought it down hard on the space just above my temple. My feet gave out and I was on the ground, gravel digging into my hands and face. I wasn't out but it was close. My vision had gone haywire and was fuzzy even in the rain and darkness. I tried to knock the cobwebs loose but it was no use.

I smelled it before it hit my skin. Lo's oxtail soup slowly at first, then all at once poured down over my head and puddled beneath my chin. Then the rice and chicken with the fat noodles. The sound of their feet began to move away from me as

I lay there, covered in my dinner trying desperately to stay awake. From above I could hear a faint meow. Boris must be in the window that looked out over the alley.

The blackness took control and I succumbed to the nothingness that was calling me. My head hit the ground and I went to sleep.

CHAPTER FIFTEEN

It didn't matter to me that the car was stolen. The only thing that counted for me was her. The nonchalance in her posture as she gripped the wheel and jerked it hard, sending screams and smoke from the tires as we spun onto Atlantic Avenue. She pressed the gas pedal to the floor and we lurched forward. A thin smile creased her lips when she saw me grip the hand rest.

Two hours earlier I was sitting on a hard wooden bench with my brother Darryl trying to figure out a way to move the truckload of boat parts he happened to be in possession of. Being fairly new to Harbor Point the connection with local fences hadn't been established yet. Besides, that was more Darryl's territory than mine and I was trying to keep off the radar. New location, new me. It wasn't going well.

It was a gorgeous summer day and the best place to be when you got weather like that was the middle of the boardwalk in the Atlantic Circle. The people watching was unrivaled and by that I mean it gave both of us an opportunity to admire the abundance of pretty girls either in bikinis coming off the beach or dressed in equally skimpy attire just strolling the boardwalk.

I sipped a tart, ice cold lemonade and tried to listen to Darryl list off his potential avenues for distribution of his hot items but I just wasn't into it. There was one sight that caught my eye. A group of girls had ascended the wooden steps from the beach, all of them glistening from a full day in the sun. At that moment I stopped listening to my brother yammering all together as my heart jumped into my throat.

At the center of these girls was one in particular that had me loopy and laser focused. The heat intensified inside my head as I became transfixed. I was being pulled into her orbit and I didn't even realize it. It wasn't her beauty although she was well stocked in that department. The soft brown skin contrasted against a bright lime green bikini top wasn't what drew me in but it was the way she held court amongst her friends and passersby.

She handled several catcalls and would be suitors with ease. She smiled and bobbed her head to some dance music that was drifting down from a rooftop bar nearby. Her overly large black sunglasses obscured her eyes and I was simultaneously intrigued and afraid to see what I would find when I looked into them. A friend passed her a joint and she inhaled deeply, without a care in the world.

I got off the bench and approached the group, weaving in and out of passing pedestrian traffic. When I got close several of the girls gave me a "here comes another one" look but I ignored them and waded directly into the center, facing the dancing enchantress.

"You think I could hit that?" I said without even realizing what I was saying, hoping I was forming actual words.

She looked to her friends and said, "That's a bit forward, don't ya think? We just met." Her friends, predictably, all laughed in unison.

I could tell she was studying me behind those saucer like glasses.

"You know what I mean."

"There's cops all over this boardwalk. You sure?"

"The last thing I'm thinking about are the cops right now."

She took one more deep hit and passed the joint to me. I gripped it between my thumb and forefinger, stuck it to my lips and inhaled hard. The smoke hit my lungs and I held it until I couldn't and blew out a long stream of smoke.

"Come have a drink with me," I blurted out as my exhale dissipated into the sky.

"Pretty basic," she said.

"You do one drink with me and then you can walk if you want."

"I can walk right now."

"Good point but if you walk now there aren't any free drinks to go along with it."

She looked at me, smiled, and began to bob her head again to the music before saying, "I don't wanna have a drink." She took two steps and pressed lips to my ear and whispered, "I've got a better idea."

The Harbor House was two blocks from the boardwalk and served as the Point's home base for an upscale dining experience. During the summer season it was packed to the gills every night with vacationers looking for something more than pizza and funnel cake.

I followed my mystery woman without giving a thought to my brother, whose anger had probably boiled over by this point. He should have been used to it by now.

We got to the front of the Harbor House. Families milled around on the wide wraparound wooden deck, trying to corral their bored and hungry children.

As we walked she said, "Go ask the valet for directions."

"Directions to where?" I said

"Fucking California. It doesn't matter," she said.

She held back as I got to the valet stand and approached a kid in an ill fitting dress shirt and black vest who looked barely old enough to operate a vehicle. Another young kid had just taken a set of keys and was getting into a waiting car.

"Hey, uh, let me ask you a question. If I wanted to walk to the marina how long would that take?" I asked, trying to look confused.

"You lookin' at a solid thirty, maybe a little more," the kid said.

I scratched my chin, feigning contemplation of his words. When the second valet pulled off in his car I asked, "And it would be that way right?" I said, pointing in the opposite direction. I was well aware of where the marina was.

He shook his head in frustration and gently grabbed me by the elbow spinning me around. I took a good five steps away from the podium he was operating and said, "So I go up this street and then what?"

He came out from behind his position and joined me. "Just take this main drag here and it'll wrap around to the left and you'll run right into it," he said.

While he was explaining this my girl brushed by us passing behind the valet's podium. She did a slight dip down and kept walking in one fluid motion. You would have had trouble spotting it even if you were looking. I thanked the valet and walked around the restaurant and we met up in the lot that served as parking for the Harbor House.

She led the way through a small sea of cars. In her hand was a set of keys. Mercedes. Her fingers pressed the button every ten feet or so until we saw the taillights on a slick cream sedan jump to life. Our pace quickened as we approached the car. The doors unlocked and we slid inside, me in the passenger seat and her behind the wheel. The ride seemed brand new.

Before she brought the engine to life she looked at me at and took her sunglasses off, revealing a set of sparkling almond eyes, full of the excitement I knew would be there.

"My name is Cherry," she said.

"I'm Ellis."

In short order Cherry had the Mercedes hurtling down Atlantic Avenue swerving around slower cars that populated the two-lane roadway. We headed out of the circle and before long were in The Bottoms. Although there was no music playing she continued to bop her head to a soundtrack only she could hear.

Several small side streets led us to a graffiti covered garage bay door. Cherry pressed on the steering wheel with her palm, compelling the car's horn.

"When we get in there just be cool. You're good with me but just keep your mouth shut," she said.

The door flew open and Cherry navigated the car into a cramped garage. It was deep. In front of us was a Cadillac carcass, splayed out in a million pieces.

This was Cherry's uncle's place. A small time chop shop that supplied an auto parts dealer up north. I said nothing as instructed but being the only white face in a garage full of guys named Stacks, Body, OBX and Knucks didn't make me feel like I was good, with her or not. As it happened somebody had recognized me from some fight and it was all good. I talked boxing while Cherry dealt with her uncle whose name was Buckshot. I could take a good guess where a name like that comes from. Buckshot was not a large man but grizzled and hard with a bald head and a stubbly gray beard. A gold tooth reflected from his mouth when he spoke. He didn't strike me as a man who had a sense of humor about many things.

We exited through a side door. I hadn't realized how hot it was in there til I stepped into the cooler air. Sweat dripped from my forehead. Cherry laughed as she reached into her shorts and pulled out a wad of cash. She split the stack and handed me half. It was a good haul for ten minutes work.

She winked at me and said, "Not bad for a first date, huh?"

We navigated the neighborhood on foot until we were out on Beach Boulevard.

"We walkin' back?" I said

"Unless you wanna grab another car?" she said, half joking. I think.

"I'm good."

Shoulder to shoulder we moved. I couldn't speak for her but there were sparks flying; a connection being made that I felt and I think she did too. She would throw an occasional look my way and I would smile awkwardly or try to make a joke.

"You stupid," she said in a playful tone.

I took her hand in mine and she didn't pull away and we walked like that for ten or twelve blocks until we came to a small corner store advertising everything from beer to tuna fish in the cramped dirty window.

"Ima get some cigarettes," she said.

"I got it," I said, leaving her on the corner. I entered the tiny store and informed the clerk, who sat behind thick bulletproof glass, which smokes I wanted. I passed a ten dollar bill into a slot through the protective glass when I heard my name. Someone was screaming and it was loud enough that I could hear it as if the person were right next to me. It was Cherry.

I moved to the door and swung it open.

CHAPTER SIXTEEN

Cherry's voice came to me through the darkness. It was raining hard and I had the violent stench of vomit in my nose. It must've came up while I was out of it. The rain came down harder than before and the combination of Chinese food, blood and puke must have given Cherry a shock because her face was stricken with panic and fear.

She knelt down and placed a soft hand on my shoulder and said, "Ellis, oh my God. What happened to you? Can you stand? We need to get you to a hospital."

The inside of my mouth was coarse and dry but I managed to whisper, "No hospital. Just get me upstairs."

Cherry did her best but all she could manage was to get me into a sitting position against the brick-wall. Boris was meowing overhead. Had he been doing that the whole time? Maybe the little fucker did care after all. I chuckled to myself at the thought.

I was alone again. Cherry had disappeared but before long she was back. I recognized Mr. Ortiz's voice as the two conversed in Spanish and they both moved in unison to get me on my feet. Once upright I managed a little stability but the pain in my side was blindingly intense. All three of us shuffled to the back stairway and with a monumental amount of trouble we ascended, step by step until we were through my back door and into the kitchen.

The light snapped on and my eyes went fuzzy from the intense shift from darkness to light. My hand gripped Mr. Ortiz's shoulder tighter to stay on my feet and he reinforced his hold on me as well. I haven't needed much help in my years here but it pays to have people that will have your back when you need it, whether you ask for it or not.

I made it through the kitchen and into the living room in one piece and as I flopped onto the couch I immediately felt the need for sleep wash over me.

"Hey hey, none of that. Keep your fucking eyes open, Ellis," Cherry said, clear and loud into my blood crusted face.

She positioned me upright and walked Mr. Ortiz out of the room. Boris hopped onto my lap and was trying to get at my face, his whiskers tickling my nose. I gently guided him to the floor but he refused this gesture and was back on the couch, this time right next to me.

My mind was slipping and it felt like an eternity before she was back in the living room and said, "We gotta get you cleaned up."

She started with my sneakers, both muddy and soaked, and worked her way up to my belt and jeans. Boris did his best to help out but he was useless in this endeavor so he mostly let meows of encouragement go at regular intervals.

Getting my shirt over my head proved the most difficult. The range of motion on my arm was gone. Cherry dashed out of the room and was back with a pair of scissors. The shirt was in pieces in no time and there I sat, in my underwear, badly hurt.

The look on her face was a mixture of sympathy and pity. She patted my knee and said, "Don't worry. You still pretty." She winked at me then got up and came back in with an assortment of supplies. Water, a bottle of aspirin, and a wash cloth. Where the hell did she find a wash cloth?

After the water and aspirin I began to regain some focus and clarity. How long was I in that alley? And Max, that fuck, would have to be dealt with in short order. My pulse began to race and I had to fight with myself to slow it down.

Cherry cleaned the gash in my hairline and wiped my face. "You gonna tell me what happened. Or should I guess?" she said as she worked.

I recounted the events from the alley. At the end she said nothing. Just looked at me with a sort of, what-did-you-expect, expression. She left and came back before she spoke again.

"I was wrong. Looks like you do have some food," she said. In her hand was a frozen bag of vegetables that I don't remember purchasing. She placed them against my grotesquely swollen ribs and I held them in place, my hand on top of hers. Like old times.

She took her hand back, looked me in the eyes and said, "You can't let those animals get their hands on that girl."

"I know. I'm gonna handle it."

"Let me help you, Ellis. Give me something to do."

"You're a hundred percent where that money is right?"

"Yeah."

"Then you did what you were supposed to do. Leave the rest to me."

"Oh fuck you, Ellis. You always do this shit to me. Mister

Weight of the World. I can handle it all. You ain't the only one with something to bring to the table here. I brought this to you, don't forget that."

She was right. Cherry was more than capable of pulling anything off that I could. It was one of those things that made me a difficult partner. I took on too much, never asked for help and if you called me on it, like she was doing now, I had a tendency to look for the door. In the ring and on the street confrontation was something I understood, welcomed even, but in a relationship, not so much.

She was pacing the center of the room mumbling to herself, trying desperately not to give me more. I placed a palm on the couch and propelled myself upward to a standing position. It was difficult and I almost stumbled forward. I grimaced through the pain as I moved across the room to face her.

"Fine. Here it is as I see it. We need a meeting place for unloading and storage. Maybe a small warehouse or something, a backhoe, a van and some police uniforms. Legit ones though. Not no costume shop shit," I said.

"You gonna let me in on the plan or just treat me like some hired gun?"

"It's your deal but remember that you came to me for help cause you knew it wasn't a solo kind of thing, right? I was perfectly fine before you came back whether you believe that or not. Now listen, there's some paperwork that needs to get done before we can go but I got someone for that. When that comes through I'll lay it on everyone and we can get to work."

She raised a skeptical eyebrow at me, "Everyone?"

"It ain't gonna be the two of us out there with shovels baby."

"Who is everyone?"

"Everyone is who I think will be best to pull this thing off without anyone ending up—"

A shot of searing pain lit up my side again. I fell to one knee and Cherry instinctively held me by the shoulder, keeping me from hitting the floor. It was crippling and the swelling was becoming grotesque.

"I need a doctor," I said.

"We can be at the ER in twenty. Where are your keys?" she asked.

"No hospitals. Cops at the hospitals. Go in the bedroom. Top drawer there's a small cigar case. Bring it here."

I moved to the couch and Cherry returned with the box. It was decorated with Cuban flags and slogans in Spanish. I flipped open the top and rifled through a small stack of trinkets and notes. A small cream colored business card found my fingers and I handed it to her.

"Call the Doc. Tell her I'm coming over."

Branson Professional Park wasn't technically in Harbor Point but it might as well have been. It sat just over the Calamity Bridge within spitting distance of the city limits. It took some doing but eventually I got some clothes on and managed my way downstairs and into the car.

We pulled into the complex and I directed Cherry to the location of the office we were looking for. The buildings were one-story brick structures that housed pediatricians, dentists, general practitioners and OBGYNs. The lots throughout the park were completely empty at this hour and we pulled up as close as we could.

Cherry helped me from the car and I leaned on her for support as we approached a door with a small sign that read, #17 - DR. LONNIE WALTERS, M.D.

The door swung inward as we reached it and Lonnie stood there in a hooded sweatshirt and sweatpants. Lonnie was in her early fifties with a brown pixie cut hairdo and fire red-rimmed glasses. All business, all of the time.

"Jesus Christ, Ellis. Get in here," she snapped.

We followed her through a small waiting area, past a reception desk and into an exam room.

"Pull your shirt up and lie down," Lonnie said.

Cherry helped me onto the table and lifted my shirt gently over my ribs. Lonnie slapped on a pair of rubber gloves and grimaced when she turned and saw me. I had witnessed that look on her face once before.

Lonnie Walters and I first met in a hospital after one of my fights. Sometimes the boxing commissions would impose mandatory hospital observation after fights depending on the severity of injuries. Toward the end of my fighting days the frequency of my trips to the hospital increased and Lonnie was always there for me. We became friends. After I came down to Harbor Point it was pure coincidence that she ended up here too. I parked her car once at the casino and we've stayed in touch ever since. I've got a doctor on call twenty-four hours a day. It comes in handy in my line of work.

Her fingers ran the length of my rib cage, poking and pressing with me wincing when it was appropriate. Cherry and Lonnie introduced themselves and made small talk while I was laid out like a slab of beef. "Two or three broken ribs," she said, turning to a cabinet behind her, "but I can't be too sure without an X-ray and since I know you won't go get one I'll do what I can."

She filled a syringe with a clear liquid from a tiny bottle and placed in on the counter while she cleaned the site of the injury with a cotton swab and alcohol.

"What is that?" Cherry said.

"This my dear," Lonnie said, holding up the syringe, "is a corticosteroid. It will rapidly reduce the swelling and give our boy here some relief. Ready?"

I nodded and Cherry turned away. She was always a bit of a baby when it came to the needles. Blood too. It was amazing she didn't pass out along with me in the alley.

My skin had been punctured so many times I had lost count. Just get it over with I thought. I stared at the long fluorescent tube lights in the ceiling until Lonnie snapped off her gloves. It didn't feel great but if it was going to help then I'd let the Doc do her thing.

"Give me a minute," Lonnie said. She exited the room through the door as Cherry came to my side to help with my shirt and get me to my feet. I leaned up against the exam table and Cherry stood next to me, her arm intertwined with mine.

"You scared me tonight," she said.

"I should feel great. You're no easy scare."

"I thought you were dead when I saw you."

"When I was out I had this crazy—"

Lonnie came through the door and tossed me a small plastic bottle with some pills that rattled around inside. "From my own personal collection so go easy," she said. I uncapped the bottle and ingested three of the small white pills.

"Thanks Doc. I'll bring you some cash next time I'm around," I said.

She waved her hand brushing the notion of payment away. Lonnie always did that. She moved toward us and took my face in her cupped hands and said, "I've said this before but I'm a doctor so I'm going to say it again. STOP FIGHTING. One of these days, Ellis. Okay. That's it. Now get out of here. I want to go home."

CHAPTER SEVENTEEN

The pizza was greasy. It was chewy and rubbery and frankly, I had a hard time getting it down. After the events of the evening I had been so hungry it didn't really matter what I was putting in my stomach. We sat on the couch in silence slowly eating the barely edible triangle slices.

The painkillers and shot the doctor had delivered were starting to work their magic as the swelling in my ribs had gone down dramatically and the aching in my head had dulled. I had never performed well on opioids and when I was boxing only took them when absolutely necessary. So it was of little shock to myself or anybody else when I blurted out:

"Does the name Savić mean anything to you?"

Cherry said nothing but her body language told me a different story. She tried hard not to move but her eyes could not stay focused on one thing, darting from the pizza in her hand to Boris curled up in his cat bed across the room and back on the pizza again. The artery in her neck began to throb as her pulse quickened.

"Why?" she asked in a timid, barely audible voice.

"It's time to spill it and tell me what you know. No more deceptions or games because I know you haven't been completely honest with me and that's okay. Because the way I look at it if I'm gonna get some money out of the deal I'm willing to overlook some stuff but when this guy picks me up off the street and threatens to kill me, and well, that's a different story," I said.

Cherry turned toward me with a very serious look on her face and said, "He did the same thing to me."

"When?" I said.

"For a while, before I came to see you, I thought someone had been following me that's why at the diner I thought I recognized him but couldn't be sure. A couple of days later I was walking to my car and there he was just leaning on the hood waiting for me."

"What did he say?"

"He wanted me to take a ride with him somewhere and that there was someone that wanted to speak to me."

"Did you go with him?"

"Hell no. I told him that if he didn't leave me alone and get the fuck away from my car I'd shoot him."

"Smooth."

"What the hell was I supposed to do? Go with him? You must be out of your mind."

"Weren't you curious about what he had to say?"

"A little but I was more concerned with staying alive. I don't know who this guy is or what he's capable of."

"My experience was similar. He was just standing there waiting for me."

Her eyes focused on me before she said, "Let me guess, you punched his lights out?"

"No, I went with him."

"Of course you did. What did he want?"

I recounted the experience at the Meridian Tower with the little office, Savić, and ultimately Kramer, which caused another involuntary spasm from Cherry's carotid. I could tell she was uncomfortable and I didn't want any more lies so I tried a subtle change of direction.

"Why didn't you tell me about this guy?"

"I don't know. I guess because I know you and figured you'd try to track the guy down and then get yourself killed."

"So you thought ignoring it was the better option?"

"I was figuring it out. Okay?" she said. Cherry rose to her feet and moved to the center of the room. She began to pace again. "I don't just move on shit. I gotta get everything lined up before I go and this was something I hadn't anticipated so I was sitting on it til I was ready to come to you."

"That ain't the Cherry I remember."

"A lot has changed Ellis. For both of us."

"Fine, you're working it out. Got it. Did you come up with something or should we just wait until he shows up and kills us both because Kramer sounded serious about that money. I don't know what he's capable of from inside but he's got at least one goon running around for him and it's a pretty safe bet there are probably more."

"I'm working on it. When everything is in order I'll fill you in."

"I deserved that."

"Doesn't feel great, does it?"

"Just get it done. We're too close to this to have it blow up. Literally."

There was no way I was going to leave this for her to mop

up. Her half truths and lies were so foul I could smell them seeping from her pores. It had become easy with her back in the picture. I was relaxed and in some aspects it felt like we got the band back together but there was one thing that was missing on my end that would never be there again: trust. I did not trust this beautiful woman standing in front of me. That disappeared in the rearview a long time ago.

Our conversation had deteriorated into nothingness. She continued to pace as I attempted to chew the last piece of tough crust from the pizza. It was bland with the texture of what I imagined cardboard would taste like. I managed to get down what was in my mouth and tossed the remaining piece in my hand onto a paper plate that was sitting on the coffee table.

My eyes followed her back and forth across the room before I said, "Listen, it's not that I don't trust you because I do but, I need to tighten this thing up. It's close and we can't afford to be on different pages. Okay?"

Her manicness subsided a bit and she stopped wearing out the floorboards. She had a look that made me want to take her to bed, broken ribs or not. The pills were really cooking through my bloodstream and I quickly abandoned the idea. It was a nice thought though, for a second.

I got to my feet and moved to her, placing my hands on her shoulders, "Just get the shit we need and I'll handle the personnel and it'll be fine. I promise, but right now I have to go to bed. You can stay if you want but my tank is empty."

Her forehead came forward and rested against mine. "I'm sorry I didn't tell you," she said. Her arm wrapped around my back, she lead me toward the bedroom. I looked back and saw Boris already up on the table going to town on the leftovers.

Cherry sat me down and gingerly pulled my shirt over my

head. Clear breath was still a difficult draw but once I was on my back it became a little easier and the pressure on my side lifted. She peeled off my shoes and socks and rolled me onto the bed.

My eyes were heavy and they began to open and close in slow, steady movements. The sheet was draped over my body and as I drifted off into a numb neverland, Cherry leaned in and kissed me deep and slow on the mouth. Our tongues touched briefly, stopping short of going deeper.

"Don't worry, Ellis. I'm going to take care of everything," she whispered as I drifted away.

Sunshine burst through the curtains as the sun made its ascent into the sky. It hit my face and my eyes had a reaction of opening and then instantly regretted that decision. It was bright and annoying. I tried to shift my head away but the sandpaper like feeling inside my mouth made sleep an impossibility. That and my bladder felt like it would burst.

Boris had made his encampment for the night between my legs on top of the sheet, basically pinning me to the bed. He was in no hurry to wake from his slumber, the feast of pizza no doubt weighing him down. I pulled my legs up and around him and slid out from under the sheet and planted my feet on the floor. My back was stiff and the instinct to stretch was curtailed by the throbbing in my side. Flexing a bit back and forth loosened my muscles enough for me to stand without pain and I stumbled into the bathroom.

After a piss that lasted what felt like an eternity I rinsed my mouth with water from the tap, sending instant relief to the drought on my tongue. I examined the gash in my hairline from

Max's gun. Fat fuck Russian I thought, as I made my way back into the bedroom. The large mirror attached to the dresser gave me a full view of the already bruising and swollen ribcage. Not as bad as it felt for sure but pretty fucked up. The worst I've ever had by far and every movement reminded me of that. I wanted to avoid the pills altogether but that seemed like an impossibility.

Through my mind I ran a checklist of things that needed to be handled one by one. I prioritized the events with feeding the gluttoness cat at the top of the list. Being the mind reader he was Boris meowed softly and rolled away from me onto his side.

I moved toward the window to raise the blinds and smacked my shinbone into a drawer, the bottom one, that was slightly ajar. The clothes inside were ruffled and spilling out. Did I leave it open? With some effort I bent to one knee and extended the drawer to its full length. I dug my hand to the bottom, sweeping it across the smooth wooden base. An uncontrollable anger and panic hit my entire body.

My gun was gone.

CHAPTER EIGHTEEN

I TRIED TO PUT THE THOUGHT OF THE MISSING GUN out of my head as I twisted the lock with my key and headed down the back steps. I had futzed around the apartment for a while trying to will myself out the door and as the hours passed the more anxious I became. There were things to accomplish and I'd bring up the gun to Cherry when I saw her. It kept creeping in though. What did she need it for? I know for a fact she had one of her own.

The pain in my head was still ever present but faded and in the background now. The gash was swollen and tender but it wasn't as noticeable being in the hairline. I opted against the pills the Doc had given me and instead took a handful of ibuprofen. I'd revisit the painkillers when I got back and was ready to shut it down for the night.

"Ellis, my friend. How are you feeling?" Mr. Ortiz's voice broke the late morning silence behind the store. I saw him by his truck, a box of peppers in his arms. I approached him and smiled, showing him I was in good spirits.

"I've been better but if it wasn't for you I might be a little worse. I want to thank you for helping me," I said.

He placed the box of produce at his feet and extended his hand. I took it in mine. He had a grave look on his face when he said, "Is getting worse you know? The crime. Every year worse and worse. Feel very bad this has happened to you. You have been such dear friend to my entire family. Anything I can do to help you know I do."

"I know and I appreciate it but I have to apologize for putting you in that position," I said. He waved his hand as if swatting a gnat from his face.

His eyes moved to my head, "Who has done this thing to you? Do you know?"

"I don't know but I'm gonna find out and when I do believe me, they won't be coming back," I said.

"Well," he said, tossing a free hand in the air, "I keep an eye out too okay. Anything smell like fish I call you. You good kid, Ellis."

He tapped me on the cheek with an open palm. I thanked him again and made my way through the alley and onto the street. It was perfect walking weather, bright and breezy. I contemplated the car but felt much more comfortable on my feet than sitting.

I hung a left and walked toward the ocean, much like I had done the day before. Was it really only yesterday that I made the trip to the marina with Butch? I passed Jenni's and thought about a pack of smokes but my lungs quickly rejected the idea.

A good kid, Mr. Ortiz had said. That phrase bounced around in my mind over and over again as I stalked through the salty ocean air, getting closer to the boardwalk. I tried to think back to the last time I could genuinely be categorized as good. The years cycled backwards until I gave up, disgusted. I had tried several times to walk the absolute straight and narrow but for many reasons the path veered right and lead me directly into a thorn bush. My fault for following it I guess. Maybe I liked the way the thorns made me feel?

Negative, self-degrading thoughts were slowly oversaturated by bright blue water, catchy island music and a boat, with my name on it. This time I thought. This time would be it. Get the score and disappear into the ether, the only record of my existence being written in the boxing record books.

I crossed Boardwalk Avenue, the small two lane street that ran parallel to the actual boardwalk, climbed three wooden steps and was on the weather beaten wooden boards. The ocean waves crashed in the distance. This part of the beach was a bit of a no man's land where Harbor Point was concerned. Located between the center of attractions and the marina so there wasn't much in the way of offerings but the sand itself was usually a less crowded part of the city. There were several multi-colored umbrellas dotting the beach with a fair number of people testing the water's edge with their feet. It was far too cold for a full dip but it was closer and closer and beach goers and sunbathers could taste the summer season like a shark tastes blood in the water.

I pushed the ideas of myself and my future away, turned right, and headed toward the Atlantic Circle.

It took twenty minutes to enter the heart of the Harbor Point boardwalk in the Atlantic Circle neighborhood. I meandered, people watched, and stopped a couple of times to catch my breath. The sights and sounds intensified as I got closer but the smell is what sent my senses into overload and hit me directly in my gut.

After a few blocks of sensory bombardment my stomach had run up the white flag and I found what I was looking for: Redbeard's Island Grill. It was a fairly new place, maybe open for a year or two at the most but it commanded a valuable piece of real estate. It must have been doing pretty well to still be here as so many others have come and gone.

There were no connections to the place for me. No owner I helped out of a jam or favors I did for a manager. They did however possess these insane jerk chicken egg roll things that I couldn't get over. As soon as I stepped inside, my hunger intensified and I took a seat at the bar. I ordered a beer from a bubbly young woman named Sage who walked on the fronts of her feet. It gave her the illusion that she was bobbing up and down when she walked. She passed a menu in my direction but I waved it away. I knew what I wanted.

Sage filled a pint glass and slid it across the bar into my open hand. A nifty trick that could have gone wrong in so many ways. She winked at me and disappeared into the back. My eyes drifted to a small screen television mounted on the back wall above the bar area. The local newscast, Harbor Point Now, was running silently on the screen with captions scrolling across the bottom. It was a typical local news show focusing mostly on traffic and weather alerts.

The cool frothy beer was going down easy and made me feel a sense of serenity. This is what is was supposed to be like, sitting at a bar on the boardwalk day drinking and enjoying myself. Instead I was limiting my breathing and looking like shit.

Sage bobbed back to the bar and grabbed the empty glass and said, "Another one, Slim?"

"Please. And the name's Ellis," I said.

Again she filled the glass, flicked her wrist and landed it in my palm with not a drop on the mahogany bar top. "This one's on me, Ellis," she said and was gone again. Despite the funky walk Sage was infectious. Big smile and personality for days. The thought of returning to Redbeard's was filed away in my memory.

As I sipped my second helping of suds a middle aged man and woman took seats at the bar, a few down from me. They were holding hands and laughing so I assumed husband and wife. Sage arrived and took their drink order. With the television muted and the music from an unseen speaker system being pumped out on low volume it was easy to hear every word they said. I wasn't trying to eavesdrop but you couldn't help it.

"I think we should go with the first one honestly. No renovations, open floor plan and all the appliances are new and it's walking distance to the beach," the woman said.

"Yeah but only one bathroom. What about the one up in Jupiter Bay? That was nice." he said.

"I think we can survive on one bathroom and Jupiter Bay is like the boonies compared to here. This is where I want to be. It's much more…metropolitan. C'mon, the kids'll love it in the summers and there's enough to do that we can be down here all the time."

The man nodded his head in a slight up and down motion before he said, "Okay then, Harbor Point it is. I'll call Judy and tell her to put an offer in."

The woman clapped her hands and threw them around his neck, planting her lips on his cheek. The man fished a cell phone out of his pocket and exited the restaurant to make the call. She turned her attention to a large frozen beverage in front of her with a giant hunk of fruit hanging off the edge of the glass. A huge smile gripped her face as she sucked hard on the straw.

I leaned in her direction and said, "Congratulations. You guys are gonna love it here. It's a beautiful city."

"Thank you so much," she said and raised her glass in my direction, "your next drink is on me. I'm celebrating!"

What I wanted to do was kick my chair back, smack the drink out of her hand and tell her to run, don't walk, to Jupiter Bay. I'd rip my shirt off and show her the swollen, bruised skin and the gap in the flesh on my scalp. I'd shoo her away like I do Boris when he's trying to steal the food from my mouth. Instead I replied with a simple, "Thank you."

The problem wasn't the city as a whole. It WAS a beautiful place with a lot to offer anyone seeking sun and fun. It is, however, a city with a long history checkered with organized crime, racially segregated neighborhoods and socio-economic policies that it's still trying to reconcile with to this day. It all added up to a seedy underbelly that simmered just on the outskirts of everything the Chamber of Commerce advertised to visitors every year. Hell, that idea of what they hand out in the brochures is what brought me here in the first place and I had no one to blame for the predicament I was in but myself. So I kept my yap shut and waited for Sage.

Her husband returned and Sage placed my food in front of me. The lady kept her word and picked up my next beer and I was happy and grateful. It would work out for her and her family I was sure. They seemed like decent people and they weren't me.

The rolls were crusty and chewy in all the right places, filled with chicken, beans, cheese and a sauce that my taste buds couldn't quite get a read on. I ate slowly and turned my attention to the silent television. A commercial for the Heaven's Gate Casino was running a promo for the schedule of big time entertainment acts that would be rolling through town that summer. A couple I thought I might even be interested in.

The advertisement ended and a beautiful blonde was on the news desk. I had to follow the slow crawl of captions below the picture. There was a slight delay and the two seemed to never be in sync as the captions lagged behind slightly.

Over her shoulder a picture appeared of a man I knew. My jaw ceased chewing and I waited for the captions to catch up. It was a photo of Andrew Kramer dressed in his orange prison garb with his inmate number stenciled over his left breast. He was staring, dead eyed, into whatever camera snapped the picture. He looked the same but his demeanor on screen was in stark contrast to the exchange I had with him a few days ago in the Meridian Tower with Savić.

The image cut away to video of a crime scene outside the house Cherry and I had visited in Steelhaven but underneath the words "found dead in his cell" and "multiple stab wounds" hung on the screen, seemingly paused as if in suspended animation. The images cycled through video clips of Kramer at trial, what looked like a homicide detective giving a press conference and ultimately landing on a still photograph of Cathy Meyer, the ex-wife and would be murder victim. Even in the simple photo her face bothered me. It was off somehow in the eyes and it unnerved me.

Then it was gone and the newscast moved on to a local traffic story. I swallowed the food in my mouth and guzzled the remainder of my beer. Kramer was dead but Savić was still out there running around. I tried to fit the two together and how it meshed with me. Not that I was itching for a confrontation with a man clearly capable of murder but it was a little underwhelming as I thought Kramer was going to have a larger role in this game. I didn't want to underestimate his reach, even from the grave, so I brushed the thoughts away and signaled Sage, who was at the end of the bar cleaning glasses.

I asked for the check but what I got in return was a slim piece of receipt paper that she placed in front of me. I turned it over and in perfect script written in blue ink was a message and a phone number. It read:

YOU GET THE NEXT ONE
SAGE

I looked up but she was gone, perhaps embarrassed by her forwardness but she didn't throw off that kind of vibe. I wasn't going to stick around and put her on the spot so I grabbed the note and jammed it in my pocket and headed for the exit. I would definitely be back to Redbeard's.

The fresh air hit my lungs and my eyes adjusted to the bright sunshine on the boardwalk. Pedestrians and beachgoers moved in all directions. My head swam a bit from the beers but it provided a respite from the pain in my head and ribs.

I purchased a pair of cheap black sunglasses from a kid at a kiosk. They didn't fit but they did the job well enough. Sunglasses weren't my thing. I had taken some heavy blows in my fighting career and my vision was a little blurred from time to time in my left eye and I didn't like putting another barrier between my already faulty vision and what I was actually looking at.

I slipped the shades on to my face and headed south toward The Bottoms.

CHAPTER NINETEEN

T H E   R E G R E T   B U I L T   I N S I D E   A S   M Y   F E E T   H I T   T H E
pavement. I was tired and I should have taken the car. Walking
almost the entirety of Harbor Point's boardwalk with broken
ribs is not advisable.

My lungs took in some air and I moved forward, past The
Cheetah Club and onto a side street that ran away from it. It
was a little too early for the club to be open but I hoped to see
Evelyn's car on the street or maybe Takeoff unloading some
equipment for his shift that night. I expected nothing and that's
exactly what I got.

The street was sun shaded and cool with the oceanfront
blocked by an abandoned storefront that would most likely
never see occupants again. Garbage and debris were strewn
everywhere. Plastic cups and bags from various fast food joints
littered each side of the street as well as what seemed to be
several trash bags dumped on the corner. It smelled as if the city
garbage route had mistakenly wiped this street from the
schedule.

That was the thing about The Bottoms: it was dirty. The

persistent grime and filth that snuck into each crevice of the neighborhood made it feel a lot worse than it was. Sure, crime was higher here than in other parts of the city but what can you expect from a neighborhood that, while technically part of Harbor Point, was treated like an annoying skin tag that just needed to be tolerated. The Pearl, on the other hand, was a much more sinister and vile place although to the naked eye or say, a couple joyriding the city looking for vacation homes, it was Beverly Hills compared to The Bottoms.

Emerging from the darkened alley I came to Brunson, waited for a car to pass, then crossed. Brunson Street was the unofficial dividing line between The Bottoms and The Pearl and served people in the know as a signpost of exactly where you should and shouldn't travel between neighborhoods.

My feet carried me onto the sidewalk that ran down another artery off Brunson, Arlington Place, the unfortunate locale of my run in with King Tito's soldiers. I hoped that I wasn't in for a repeat situation as I was in worse shape defensively than I had been before.

I didn't know exactly where I was going or what to look for as I took in the small, two storied row houses that lined the street. Tiny concrete front stoops jutted out from the houses like the amusement piers stretching into the ocean from the boardwalk. I walked, figuring there were already eyes on me and before I ventured too deep into Tito's kingdom they would come to me. I wasn't wrong.

Halfway down the block a screen door opened outward and a woman, tall with a round mess of brown hair, descended the porch steps and made a beeline right for me. For a moment I thought she may walk right through me but made an abrupt stop roughly six inches from where I had planted my feet. Her dark chocolate eyes swept my features. She studied my face as I, in turn, studied hers. She looked as if she could have starred in one of those Spanish language soap operas that I used to see on television as a kid. Except for a long, zig-zagging scar that ran the length of her face from the bottom of her ear to the tip of her chin, she was a stunner.

"I need to speak to Tito. Can you make that happen?" I said.

She laughed and said something in Spanish under her breath before she responded, "You should go now. Turn around and leave before you end up with no hands." Her eyes never left mine and I did not doubt her sincerity but I wasn't leaving without seeing the King, hands or not.

"I appreciate your concern," I said and waved a hand in the air, "but I must speak with him. It's a family matter."

"What are you talking about gringo?" she said.

"It's about his niece," I said.

Her entire face focused on me, if that was possible. Her lips pursed and her eyebrows were pulled in toward the center of the face as her forehead creased with concern. She took two steps back and tucked each of her hands under the opposite arms.

"What do you know about Alana?" she said in a defiant and aggressive tone.

"What I have to say about Alana I say to Tito, not you. The only thing I will say is that this is about her safety and if you care about that, which it clearly looks like you do, you will drag your ass back in that house and call whoever you need to call so I can get a minute with the man," I said.

Her face loosened a touch and she released the fold in her arms and brought them to her side. Her voice was softer when she relented and asked, "What's your name?"

"Ellis. He'll know."

With that she turned and went back into the house, taking the three steps up to landing in one giant leap before disappearing the way she came.

This woman knew Alana and not in the way everyone in the neighborhood knows King Tito's niece. Her reaction told a different story. One that lead me to believe this woman was either a cousin, older sister or maybe even her mother. She looked a little too young for that but that didn't mean it wasn't possible.

I waited. The neighborhood was quiet and a soft breeze ran down the street, tucked neatly in between the row houses that lined each side. It felt good when it grazed the back of my neck.

Before long the woman was out of the house and again standing in front of me. She instructed me to head down to the corner and wait for someone to pick me up. I thanked her and started my move toward the end of the block.

"Is she in trouble?" the woman asked, concern lacing her words.

I turned and smiled, "Not if I can help it."

I endured some strange looks while I stood on the corner. Several passersby shook their heads at me while one elderly woman gripped her Rosary beads and said a prayer in hushed tones as she passed. It took five minutes before a sleek black Mercedes pulled up next to the curb. From inside the car a driver motioned me to get in.

I entered the car through the rear passenger side door. Inside were the driver and a thin man, who wore pressed khaki pants and a bright white t-shirt. The thin man sat next to me. He held a black cloth in his hands that he was twisting and rolling between his calloused and tattooed fingers.

"Put this on," he said in heavily accented English.

I unfurled the cloth in my hands and realized it was small bag. Not that I was comfortable putting this thing over my head but what was I going to do? Over my head the bag went and I was plunged into darkness.

The car took off from the curb and from the jolting of my body it seemed as if there were several turns, some backtracking and perhaps a loop de loop in there for good measure. The inertia from the car had my body sliding all over the back seat and at one point I felt the thin man's hand against my shoulder. My head was jumbled and if they were trying to confuse my sense of direction, they had nailed it.

We came to an abrupt stop and my head crashed into the headrest of the passenger seat. I could hear my companions laughing as I rubbed my nose through the bag. They were having a bit of fun with a white boy who didn't belong in their neighborhood. I wasn't going to hold it against them.

I heard voices coming from outside the car, a lot of them. The thin man opened his door and closed it. A second later my door was opened and a bony hand gripped my elbow and led me from the vehicle. On instinct I extended a hand in front of me feeling in the darkness. Laughter erupted around me. Hands pressed on my shoulders and pushed me forward. I stumbled and tried to hold my balance. I fell to one knee to keep from crashing onto my face. My breath was labored and my ribs began to throb again, the relief of the beer beginning to wear off. Again, a hard pair of hands came under my arms and lifted me to a standing position. The bag was ripped from my head and light flooded my vision. The pupils dilated and my eyes fought for focus.

Before I regained full power in my eyes a voice broke through the fuzziness. "I told you to call, Ellis? Why are you here?" the voice said. It was King Tito and he sounded annoyed at the very least. He was right, he did tell me to call but not only did I not have his number but the last time I looked gang leaders were not readily available in the phone book.

The haze from the sudden rush of light dissipated and I saw Tito clearly. He was sitting at a makeshift table, an elderly man to his right and a large brown and white bulldog at his feet. He was staring at me with serene calmness, no anger was present on his expression or in his eyes. I looked around. I was in a courtyard of some kind with the rear of several buildings that created a joining of backyards into a square layout. There were people around me, all as expressionless as Tito. A rough looking group, covered in black tattoos from their torsos to their faces. I focused my attention back to the King.

"We need to talk. In private," I said.

King Tito took me in, the tanned leather like skin around his mouth turned a small frown. He slid his chair back and rose, stepped over the round mass of bulldog at his feet and approached me.

Before he could speak I jumped in and said, "If it wasn't important you think I'd be here?"

"I would hope not," he said in a soft, whisper like tone.

"It's about Alana," I said, reiterating something he already knew. "Just five minutes."

"Okay, Boone, you got yourself five minutes. Follow me."

Tito brushed past me and I followed him through his gang of disciples, all of them to a man shooting daggers at me from their eyes. I recognized the two men I had the fight with out on Arlington the first time I entered Tito's territory. They looked away.

There was a smooth motion to Tito's walk as if he was gliding above the pavement. I had not quite figured out what I was going to say or in what order I would relay the events that brought me to him. We approached a small alleyway between the two story brick houses. Tito stopped and extended a hand allowing me to enter first.

"I hope you understand the danger you've put yourself in," Tito said.

I turned and nodded, never breaking eye contact. I gave him everything from the details of my relationship with the Ukrainians to Alana's photograph arriving under my door. I recounted as much of the attack by Max as I could remember but when I tried to lift my shirt and show the bruised and swollen injuries he waved me off, showing no interest. Tito's face was something akin to concrete with the only reaction coming anytime I mentioned Alana's name. The small crows feet outside his eyes would flex and tighten causing three tiny teardrop tattoos just below his left eye to do a subtle dance on his face.

"Thank you for bringing this to my attention. Alana is very important to me...to all of us. I'll have someone drive you back," he said and turned to exit the alley. I shouldn't have been caught off guard by this but I was. Besides, I had another piece of business I needed to discuss with him.

"Wait a sec, is that it?" I blurted out. He came back around to face me and got uncomfortably close to me. When he spoke his breath smelled of a mixture of menthol cigarettes and garlic. It was kind of nice.

"You gave me the information and I will act on it appropriately. I already thanked you. What more could you want?" he said, now more hiss than whisper.

"I need a piece," I said.

Tito took two steps back and took a deep breath before he said, "You don't have one? A guy like you with the people you run with? I highly doubt that."

"Mine grew two legs overnight and walked away."

"Okay Boone, I'll have it dropped off at your place tonight. It'll be clean when you get it but if it should find some dirt while in your possession...well, that has nothing to do with me."

CHAPTER TWENTY

Evelyn's busted junker was in the lot adjacent to the Cheetah when I returned, as was Takeoff's pickup. I could kill two birds with one stone and head back home to meet Tito's guy for the dropoff. Having a gun never appealed to me but with the amount of heat swirling around I felt better knowing one would be there if I needed it.

The bouncers didn't show up til much later in the evening when the drunks rolled off the beach and the bachelor parties from the casino started calling for shuttle service so there was no Reggie for me to deal with.

I paid my admission and entered into the main club area. Sparsely populated, the main stage was occupied by an anorexic looking white girl with some poor tattoos placed in all the wrong places. She was pretty but the ink made her look trashy. At this hour the club was overrun with the so-called "second team" of girls.

As Ms. Skin & Bones made her rounds to the handful of willing customers that lined the stage, I made my way to the DJ booth that rose slightly above everything else, even the main stage. Takeoff was setting up by stacking crates of records and plugging in various cables that would take me two years to decipher. Takeoff was a good kid and his eyes lit up when he saw me.

"Yo Boone! What's good, baby?" he said loudly, extending his hand. His head was in constant rhythm with the beat. The kid was always bouncing around.

I took his hand in mine, pulled him close and gave him a pat on the back and said, "Tryin' to stay alive."

"I bet," he laughed. He knew me pretty good.

It had been a long day already and I wanted to keep the small talk to a minimum so I got right to it. "Listen, I think I got something that may interest you."

"You know I'm down. Anything for you, Boone."

"Good. Your pops still have that excavating company?"

"Of course. The old man is gonna die on one of those machines waiting for me to change my mind and take over the business," he said as he moved some more records around on the turntable.

"What are the odds I can get my hands on a back hoe for a day? There'll be a nice chunk for you when it's over."

"Not a problem. But…"

"But what?"

Takeoff stopped his steady head bobbing and looked me in the eye and said, "I don't wanna be just the equipment guy anymore. I want in on whatever you're cooking."

There it was. Sometimes all you gotta do is drop the line in the water. Sure, I knew he would have said yes if I asked him straight up but if he comes out with it and shit goes bad there's no one to blame but himself. He was a willing volunteer now.

"Bigger cut I assume?" he asked.

"Always a bigger cut for those who dirty the hands," I said.

Takeoff smiled and his body went full movement now, in lock step with the beat pounding from the speakers lined throughout the club. "How much we talkin'," he asked.

"I'm a hit you up in the next day or so. We'll meet and I'll lay it all out for you."

"Bet. Good lookin', Boone. I could use the scratch man. Spinning records for Primo is getting to be a bit much. Ever since he took over the club it's gotten worse and worse."

"If the thing comes off the way I think it will you can tell Primo to go fuck himself."

"That's what I wanna hear, man."

"Where's Evelyn? I saw her car out front but I haven't seen her."

"She's in the back getting ready. She's going on after the next girl. Bout ten or fifteen."

"I'm gonna get a drink. I'll be in touch."

Takeoff nodded and smiled. I moved over to the bar and took a seat facing away from the stage. I contemplated a gin and tonic but thought better of mixing the booze in my belly and opted for a bottle of beer instead. I never ordered a draft beer from a strip club, especially one as seedy as The Cheetah. I would bet those tap lines haven't been cleaned since the seventies.

The music changed and Takeoff announced the next dancer. I turned, beer in hand, to check out the next girl. My eyes followed her from the dressing room to the small set of steps and then onto the stage. She went straight for the pole and hoisted herself toward the ceiling. That's all I managed to see as my gaze fell on a patron sitting at the stage conversing with Ms. Skinny. My face must have revealed my shock as I was staring at Wheels himself, with a stack of cash piled in front of him and a giant white bandage that covered his right hand. How could that be? In all my time dealing with Roman and Max I never saw anyone I dealt with again. I assumed they either skipped town, paid their debt and peeled off or ended up on the specials menu at the Kitchen.

I slid off my stool and walked around the back wall away from where Wheels had his attention. I didn't want him to see me coming. As I stalked, Ms. Skinny caught my approach and made eye contact with me which in turn caused Wheels to glance over his shoulder. He did a double take, a blend of disgust and fear flashed across his face. He swung his massive body around in the chair and held up his bandaged hand. A literal white flag.

I, on the other hand, was genuinely happy to see him. Despite our run-in I could have cared less who Wheels gave the rip to or how much he was spreading around while he owed everyone and their mother. His look said he did not reciprocate the feeling.

From my pocket I pulled a wad of cash and peeled of a fifty, handing it to Ms. Skinny and said, "I need to talk to this guy for a second." Her reflexes were remarkable as the bill was gone before the words fell from my mouth. I slid into the plush leather chair next to Wheels and smiled.

"What the fuck do you want? I don't want no shit aight?" he said, not in a confrontational tone but more matter of fact. I felt the same. If Wheels and I got into it right now it wouldn't be pretty, for either of us.

"Fair. I'm not here to mix it up I swear," I said and I showed him my palms as a peace offering, "but I'm very curious as to how you are sitting here right now? Spill it." I could tell he didn't want to explain himself but my eyes let him know there was no choice in the matter. He rolled his eyes, defeated.

"Will you leave me the fuck alone then?" he asked.

"Maybe," I said.

"Whatever. After that shit outside which ain't never happened to me before by the way—"

"Ah don't feel bad, Wheels. I'm a trained professional."

"Yeah, so I found out later. Anyway, after I woke up, they worked me over and smashed my fucking hand with a hammer. Max laid some twenty four hours shit on me so I went out and boosted what I owed them and we're square."

"That's it?"

"Yeah that's it. What the fuck else you want from me?"

He looked away from me and took a deep swig from the beer bottle in front of him, emptying it.

"You want another one? It's on me," I said.

He shot me an are-you-serious look. Can't say I blamed him in that moment. It wasn't personal and while I sat there watching this giant man feel humiliated, I had an idea. A bit of charity welled up inside me and I said, "Can you still drive with that hand all busted up?"

"I could drive with no hands, bro."

"I'm in the market for a driver. You interested?" I said. Wheels didn't respond. He just stared straight ahead at nothing in particular. He was at least listening.

"Let me make it up to you. I'm out with those crazy fucks and whatever you wanna believe, what happened between me and you was pure business. You of all people have to understand that. I'm just tryin' to get paid like everyone else out here. But what if I told you that I could end the hustle and put enough green in your pockets that you could move into the fucking Champagne Room if you wanted."

The new girl on stage slid over to us and began gyrating in the typical erotic dancer fashion. You could tell she was just cycling through the series of moves she had learned and that was it. That's what you get before midnight, I thought. She made eye contact with me and smiled. I reached over and grabbed a dollar bill from Wheel's pile and handed it to her. She took the cash and slid it behind her onto the stage. Wheels accommodated her with a handful of dollars, each one slid to a different part of her body. This was his thing I guess. Some people liked knitting, Wheels liked giving his money to strippers. Who was I to judge?

"How much we talking?" he said as our dancer slithered away to another customer. He was looking at me now.

"A lot. If you're in, we'll meet, and we can run it down."

After a minute or two of hard contemplation Wheels agreed to be my driver. I took his number and told him I'd be in touch. He said a hearty, "Fuck you," as I walked away. I deserved that.

I doubled back to the bar and ordered another beer and had one of the girls get Wheels whatever he wanted. I took my beer and grabbed a seat at the stage waiting for Evelyn, or Cocoa Brown, to get on the stage.

The music changed to a more seventies vibe with a modern beat layered underneath it. Takeoff got on the mic and informed all in attendance that, "The Queen, Miss Cocoa Brown was gracing us with her luxurious presence and to get those dollar bills ready."

Evelyn erupted from the dressing room with a skin tight, full bodied crimson lingerie gown with a train that trailed behind her. She hit the stage in step with the music and immediately injected life into the dull club atmosphere. Although Evelyn was on the back nine of her career looks wise she made up for that and then some with experience. She was the consummate pro on stage, knew all the moves and employed them effortlessly. Watching her up there was a thing of pure art which not many women could pull off without looking like a fool but the only thought in my mind was that hopefully, if all broke right, Miss Cocoa Brown would be hanging up her stripper pumps for good very soon.

I drained my beer as Evelyn got to me. Anytime I was in here, which was rare, she never took my money. Just did a little show and moved on. That was until Primo took over the club because in his eyes a customer that doesn't pay isn't a customer. I suspected for a while that Primo tried to get rough with her but she would never tell me that. Evelyn could handle herself and getting me involved in anything like that was a last resort for her. She always tried to protect me from the big bad men of Harbor Point.

The red get-up had been discarded and she was now fully nude. She reached out her arm, grabbed my shoulder and pulled me in close. Her skin smelled of perfume and sweat. I slid a dollar onto the stage to keep up appearances.

"What're you doing down here? Slumming?" she asked.

"It builds character. You should try it sometime," I said and pulled my face from her bosom and looked her in the eyes.

"Sugar, I live it, you know that," she said with a devilish smile.

"How 'bout I relieve you of that burden?"

"And how you gonna do that?"

Now it was my turn to smile. I reached into my pocket and pulled out a crisp one hundred dollar bill. I gripped it between my index and forefinger and ran the Ben Franklin along her dark mahogany skin slowly, from just below her belly button, over her stomach and came to a stop directly between her soft breasts. I looked her in the eyes and peered into her soul.

"With a shitload of these."

CHAPTER TWENTY-ONE

I SAT IN THE DARK APARTMENT LOST IN MY OWN HEAD. Boris was asleep on my lap and I smoked the small black cigarettes that Cherry must've left the last time she was here. Boris purred relentlessly as I stroked his ears and the back of his neck.

The phone went directly to voicemail when I dialed Cherry's number and I couldn't help think that she was out there doing bad things with a gun that was registered in my name. It wouldn't be beyond her and I certainly knew what she was capable of. It sent a shiver through my body and Boris, clearly annoyed at the slight movement, hopped to the floor and voiced his displeasure. He made his way to the cracked window and promptly wedged himself into the small opening.

Regardless of what Cherry was doing the plan was progressing. Only a visit to my contact in the City Hall was needed and the big components would be in place. The rest would iron itself out as we moved forward. The cigarette emitted a harsh orange glow in the blackness. I took another drag and finished it off, extinguishing it in the ashtray.

Now I waited for Tito to deliver my piece of mind. Once that came the plan was to drive over to the Meridian Tower and see if I could pick up the trail for Savić and see what this guy was up to now that Kramer was out of the way. I slid down on the couch and rested my aching head against the cushion, my eyes becoming heavy.

A noise from the alley jolted me upright without thinking, sending searing pain once again rippling through my torso. It sounded like muffled voices. Boris's fur was puffed out and on all ends and he was meowing in an almost uncontrollable manner. A shout and more muffled voices followed.

I got up from the couch and strode to the window, swatting Boris with one hand while lifting the window with the other. My neck craned against the screen attempting to get a look at the alley below. I could only see the top of my car but otherwise the alley seemed empty. Strange, I thought. I pulled my body from the sill but a low groan caught my ear. I gripped the levers on the screen and hoisted it upward, jutting my head out into the cool evening air. There was a body slumped face down at the mouth of the alley closest to the rear of the building.

I slammed the screen shut so Boris wouldn't launch himself out the window, slid my sneakers on my bare feet and ran to the back door. I took the back stairs three at a time and hit the ground at a run. I made it two feet and stopped dead. I recognized Mr. Ortiz's white chef's coat in a heap on the ground, blood streaming from his head. Sprinting to his side, I dropped to my knees and inspected the damage to my friend.

Blood boiled through my veins as my hands instinctively moved to his head. I tried not to move him in a way that would cause further damage. A flap of skin hung away from his skull and the blood leaked down his face and onto the ground, pooling around his mouth. I yanked the t-shirt from my body and gently pressed it against the ghastly wound. His back moved in a slow, labored up and down motion so at least I could see he was alive.

"Fuck," I said to no one in particular. I had to get to a phone. I had left my cell on the kitchen table upstairs so I decided to leave Mr. Ortiz for a moment and go into the restaurant and call the emergency hotline. My shirt was already soaked in blood resulting in a wet black mess.

I rose to my feet and heard the rapid crunching of gravel behind me. Before I could turn, a powerful arm slipped around my neck securing me against the chest of my assailant. The forearm closed quickly against my throat cutting off any oxygen I attempted to take in. It hit my nose before the rag like material covered my mouth. It was akin to disinfectant but possessed a fruity quality as if you combined glass cleaner with red wine, rum and unwashed wet towels. The dampness pressed against my mouth and I tried hard not to breathe in but it was beyond impossible. My head began to swim with disorientation when I felt a sharp pain in my neck as if my skin was jabbed with a hot poker.

As the light faded from my consciousness I saw Mr. Ortiz's motionless body on the ground. My brain tried to send a message to my arm to reach out but there was no answer and I faded into the oblivion of my own mind, knowing and feeling nothing.

Bone chilling cold. That's what woke me up. I think. My vision fluttered through a soft unfocused haze. My hands were bound by tight zip ties and latched to a hook extending down from the ceiling. Blood trickled along my extended arms where the ties dug into the frozen skin. Shifting back and forth was a necessity as my height would not allow a flat footed stance.

The puncture wound in my neck throbbed and the searing pain along my ribcage was intensified ten fold due to the forced extension of my torso. My head was swimming from whatever chemical concoction was forced into my system.

The fog lifted from my vision and I knew exactly where I was. In almost the same spot that I dangled from was where Roman and I conversed over Vanya's corpse. I could almost see Roman then, a ghostly vision. That image was quickly replaced with a thought of Mr. Ortiz, slumped over in the alley. I hoped he was alive.

Maybe I was hallucinating. I shook the thought of my friends away and tried to regain focus. I was in a long shot position for survival and if there was a chance to come out of it alive, I needed my wits.

Several black body bags filled tables that ran along each wall, some larger than others but all full. In a corner was a tall stack of folded, but as of yet unoccupied, identical bags. The cold ripped through me to the bone as my teeth rattled around in my head, my breath visible with each exhale.

There was movement just outside the door as shadows danced on the drab gray concrete floor. I extended my toes, getting up as high as I could and slid my wrists back and forth in quick, successive bursts running the edge of the zip tie along the round extension of the hook. The hard plastic dug deeper and deeper into my flesh with no identifiable difference to the integrity of the ties. My legs, overwhelmed with exhaustion, gave out and my body hung limp. I thought my hand might be severed if I remained like that and just enough strength was mustered to get back to a standing position.

The door swung open and in stumbled Max. He looked terrible but then again he never looked good. The grin that spread wide across his face was in direct opposition to his physical appearance. He shuffled over to me, almost close enough to smell the fear building inside. Before he spoke I got a whiff of the cigarettes on his breath and the cheap vodka seeping from his pores. Max reached into his pocket and pulled one of those cigarettes from a box and lit up, blowing smoke into my face. I coughed hard sending a fresh jolt of pain up my side.

"Not so tough now Mister Fighting Man," Max said. He was right. Even if they cut me down there wasn't much I could do. I turned away as Max blew yet more smoke into my face, burning my eyeballs.

"Where's Roman, Max? He in one of these bags you sick fuck," I said.

He grabbed a folding chair that was against the wall, set it up in front of me and took a seat, crossing his legs as much as he could manage. He smoked for a while, not saying anything. He just smiled that dumb smile.

"What is it they say?" he said, "America is land of opportunity, yes? I always have hate for you but who would know that you would be that opportunity for me?"

I had no clue what this dumb troll was yammering about and the thought crossed my mind to hoist myself up and dropkick him in the chest. He was open for it but I had no move beyond that so I nixed the idea. Then Max said something not so dumb and my fear went to another level.

"Ellis Boone. Treasure Man," he said with a laugh. He rose to his feet and pressed the smoldering cigarette into my chest, burning the flesh. I took a deep breath and dealt with the pain the best I could. "I told you, yes? You leave in pieces from this place. This my promise to you," he growled. He dropped the cigarette on the ground, stamped it with his foot and exited the room.

I was on the verge of sensory overload. Treasure Man? What the fuck was he talking about? There was no way these guys knew about the money unless they got to Cherry. Was she even on their radar? The questions proposed themselves faster than I could answer them.

The door swung open again, two men entered and then I understood exactly the meaning behind Max's words. Savić, followed from behind by Max, approached me. His eyes sparkled behind the dark rimmed glasses that rested on his nose. The room began to feel very small, as if the walls were closing in around me. The giant Ruslan entered a few seconds later mashing his giant paws together, eager to put them to work. He moved in line next to Max and the three of them gawked at me with a mixture of scowls and smiles but all looking like hungry wolves about to eat.

Savić gripped my chin in his hand and turned my head from side to side, inspecting my features. He released my face and ran his palm along my neck, over the puncture and down my chest to the charred flesh from Max's cigarette. He smiled and inserted a finger deep into the tender spot. My teeth bore down on themselves as I committed to not crying out. That's what he wanted. He removed his finger, took a step backward and wiped his hand on his pants.

"I believe, and correct me if I am wrong, Mr. Boone, that the last time we had the pleasure of each other's company I did indeed warn you about everything that is happening right now," he said as he slid into Max's abandoned folding chair. "You have no one to blame but yourself."

An attempt to twist from his grasp was futile so I shot back, "What happened? You lose your master? Kramer kicks and you throw in with this lot? Like a little puppy dog looking for a new owner."

He turned to Max who smiled a wide drunken smile. When he returned his gaze to me he was also smiling and said, "I think you have drastically misunderstood the nature of our relationship." He stepped back and snapped a finger in Ruslan's direction. The big bear of a man moved on me, uncorking a devastating right hand that if it had landed square would have shattered my jaw. Instead, his fist connected somewhere just below my eye. The lights in my consciousness began to blink on and off with black spots dotting my vision.

"You speak only when spoken to," growled Ruslan whose English accent was markedly better than Max's. As I grasped at any semblance of composure Ruslan took his place and Savić once again stepped forward.

"But it is not your fault, Mr. Boone. Kramer did not understand his role either and he has paid the ultimate price for his..." Savić said, trailing off as if searching for the right words before he continued. "No matter. You will now be fulfilling the late Mr. Kramer's duties. So I will ask you a question. A very important question that requires a precise answer and I implore you to take your time and think about your reply very carefully because it will only be uttered once. You will not be leaving this room intact if the answer is not to my liking. Are we in agreement on this?"

I wasn't leaving this room alive either way so what did it

matter. Deliberately, I nodded my head in agreement. Savić leaned forward until his mouth was positioned just outside my ear and hissed, "Where is the money, Ellis? What plot is it in? Tell me now and I promise that you will suffer no more."

There existed a level of pain when I would tell these guys anything they wanted to hear. The money, that's what this was about? Confusion moved in permanently as I attempted to run through what was happening. Was Kramer holding out on Savić? How could he not know where the money was? A larger problem presented itself with the speed of a freight train. I didn't know where the money was either. I had never pressed Cherry on the issue knowing she would never tell me until it was time. Even if I wanted to I couldn't give these guys what they wanted.

An unintentional laugh escaped from behind my lips and immediately Ruslan stepped forward to thrash me again but Savić held up an arm to intervene. Was it possible to be grateful to a man you knew was about to end your life?

"You laugh as if you have something to laugh at. Enlighten me," he said with the patience of a saint.

I gathered my self and said, "What's funny is that this whole time you've been running around the city doing Kramer's bidding and God knows what else just hoping that he would tell you where it was? Sounds like a piss poor plan to me, boys."

Now it was Max's turn to jump on me but Savić barked something in Ukrainian and Max retreated like a scolded pet. I had never seen Max react like that before and a new wave of fear washed over me.

"It would have been ideal for him to reveal the location but he is a trying man as you have seen. When you presented yourself as an alternative Mr. Kramer's involvement no longer became necessary. So, here we are then. Your answer, please."

"Why would I tell you anything? If you're going to kill me anyway what's the incentive? What's in it for me," I asked legitimately, attempting to angle for a sliver of hope.

"The magnitude of where you sit has not sunk in yet has it, Mr. Boone? It is true I am going to end your life one way or another, whether you give me what I require or not. What you can control is the manner and speed at which you die. Tell me where the money is and once it is secured Max will put a bullet through your skull. It will be the right way. After all, I am a charitable man when need be. Mislead or refuse and you get the flame until you break and give me what I seek—and then you get the flame until you die."

"Is there a third option?"

"You are a peculiar man, Mr. Boone. Peculiar indeed. As it happens there is a third choice and you are ever so close to triggering it. If you manage to expire without divulging what is mine I will get it from your little girlfriend," Savić hissed again, his hands moving back and forth over one another.

"You motherfuck—"

"And when she breaks, which she will most certainly do, she will have a home in Kiev. Black skin. Exotic. Will be in very high demand."

Max and Ruslan laughed in unison while Savić never broke eye contact. He was reveling in the anguish that was oozing from my spirit. In that moment I never wanted to take a life more than that. I could picture his blood as my pulse raced. Paranoia quickly took the place of rage.

"Okay, okay listen and what I am going to tell you is one hundred percent the truth," I half pleaded, "I have no earthly clue where that fucking money is man and she doesn't either. We couldn't find it."

Max spat towards me and screamed, "Lying fuck pig!"

"Have you ever been tortured before, Mr. Boone?" Savić said, eyeing my physique, "No I think not. It is an unpleasant experience of which there is no equal. Depending on the manner of course."

Savić raised his mangled nub of a hand and showcased it to me. It was pink and smooth with splotches of dark red and scar tissue seemingly sewn directly into the surface. In reality Savić was only missing two whole fingers and part of another but it was gross to the eyes.

"Many tears were shed that day I tell you," he said with a grim and solemn look on his face, "and now you will know that pain." Savić snapped his fingers on his good hand at Ruslan, who promptly headed for the door and slipped out of the room.

Savić removed his sport coat, draped it over the chair and began to roll his sleeves up to the elbow. I turned my attention to Max, who was watching Savić with a reverence in his eyes. Who was this guy?

"And what about the girl, Max? All that piss and venom over the girl and for what? Was any of that real or were you just fucking with me?" I said in a voice I could barely muster.

"World not always revolve around you. I have plan for little bitch girl. After I cut her uncle's head off she will suck the cocks of our comrades for the rest of her worthless life," he said with a laugh as he took a step in my direction, "and there not one thing you can do."

The last syllable dribbled from Max's lips when all three of our heads snapped towards the door. It was a hard thud combined with a short, quick shout. Then there was silence save for the soft whirring of the refrigeration unit. Savić snapped something at Max in Ukrainian.

Max pulled a snub nosed pistol from his jacket and marched toward the door like a dutiful little soldier. It happened so fast I had difficulty processing what my eyes were taking in, like an alternate reality that I couldn't quite comprehend.

In one fluid motion Max gripped the handle and pulled. At the precise moment the door passed his body, opening him up to the outside room his chest exploded in a glorious spray of blood and bullets. Four to be precise. Max stumbled and shuffled and choked on his own blood, eventually ending up on his face gasping for his final hints of life.

Savić, with a bit more life in his step than I thought the old man could manage, sprung forward and came to rest just behind the steel door. He ripped a small firearm from an ankle holster, spun and fired wildly three times through the doorway. The intense sound of the gunfire reverberated inside the small room and created a tiny buzz in my ears.

Desperately I rocked my body back and forth hoping to make some headway on the restraints that held me to the ceiling. Savić unloaded the remainder of his bullets through the doorway. His chest was heaving and the sweat poured from his brow. Then came the fatal mistake. He slid his body along the ground to the edge of the door and popped his head around for a peek.

BANG!

Chunks of flesh and skull were ripped from his head and landed on the floor with a full splat as if someone dropped a watermelon on the ground.

Now it was my turn to sweat. As I made a futile last ditch

effort to wriggle myself free my eye caught the glint of a large silver gun.

I closed my eyes and silently made peace with the bullet that had my name on it.

The footsteps were soft as they approached, almost silent. Adrenaline started to build and I took a deep breath in and held it. A drum line played a beat as my eardrums pounded in rhythm with my heart until the touch of soft skin ran along the small of my back. I was being spun around. From beneath a squinted eyelid I snuck a look and saw a bright flash of pink below. I opened both my eyes.

Bright pink high top converse sneakers, jeans ripped at the knees and a large handgun cradled so naturally as if it was an extension of the arm. Alana stared at me emotionless, her brown eyes focused on the welts, bruises and cigarette burn that littered my face and torso.

"Are you okay?" she asked in a whisper.

I said nothing. I stared at this young girl and let the raw emotion of the moment storm over me. Then the tears came and there was no defense against it. Alana dragged the empty chair close, pulled a small four inch folding knife from her pocket and cut me down. My body collapsed on the floor, my legs no longer possessing the strength required.

The blood rushed back into my arms creating a sensation that was equal parts pleasure and pain. I stretched and flexed my fingers in and out until the tingling abated and the feeling returned.

"Come, we must go now if you can," Alana said, placing a hand below my armpit and lifting me the best she could to my feet. It was shaky but Alana threw my arm over her shoulder and wrapped her own around my waist. She led and I followed. We maneuvered around and over the lifeless, bloodied bodies of Max and Savić, careful to not step in the growing pools of dark crimson blood.

In the outer room I saw the fate that had befallen Ruslan. His body was crumpled at the foot of the stairs, his extremities contorted in almost comical directions. His face appeared to have exploded from the inside out. A gunshot to the back of the head would do that.

"You good? I don't think I can carry you up," she said, catching her breath.

"I think I'm okay," I lied. Reaching for the railing, I steadied myself. Alana went up first and I followed with great duress. We moved through the back room and out the rear door into the steamy humid air. The sweat on my body intensified and if not for Alana's reflexes, I would have hit the ground.

We moved slowly, probably slower than she would have liked but eventually exited onto a street that ran along the back of the lot that the Ukrainian Kitchen occupied. Alana pointed up the street to an idling white van under the soft white glow of a street lamp.

She reached the vehicle, grabbing the handle on the side and throwing the sliding door open and when I reached the opening I saw the driver behind the wheel, wearing a baseball cap pulled down low. King Tito turned and beckoned me inside.

CHAPTER TWENTY-TWO

It's amazing what a bit of food, a hot shower and a handful of painkillers can do. I dropped into bed and Boris was immediately on me, purring manically and rubbing the corners of his mouth against my hands. His affection was nice and what I needed at that moment. His body twirled in circles until he found a spot he liked and plopped himself directly on my hip. The warmth he gave off was soothing.

My recollection of the night's events were already fading in and out and my ability to separate fact from fiction became more difficult the more I pondered it. Partly, I think, because it was so traumatic and I guess it might be the brain rejecting the notion that it was so close to death.

Images, like old Polaroids, flashed in my mind's eye. Max and Savić piled on top of each other, their blood turning the floor black. Ruslan and his distorted facial features would probably have an effect on my dreams for the rest of my life. Then there was Alana. I thought of her face as she led me from that basement. When I was an up and coming fighter a journalist once described me as having the killer instinct required to become a champion. Peering into her eyes showed me what it really looked like.

After she helped me into the van and we were on our way back to Harbor Point I tried to speak, to express some gratitude. My mouth was dry and hoarse but before I could get any words out Tito held up a hand from the front and that ended any attempt at conversation.

I rested my head against the window, closed my eyes and drifted off as we merged onto the highway. When I awoke we were just entering the area for the Harbor Point exits. There were three of them: the Casino/Marina District, Atlantic Circle-City Center and Downtown, each of them dumping you off at a different point along Atlantic Avenue.

The fact that we were heading off the highway towards the Casino/Marina was a bit of a surprise but I wasn't going to chance a comment from the back seat. Tito navigated through several traffic lights and pulled into the large parking lot across the access road to the marina. It was almost pitch black save for a dim street light just outside the rusted chain link fence.

Minutes passed in silence until a dark silhouette emerged from the dock area. The figure approached, waited for a passing car before crossing the street into the lot and made a beeline for our position. It was a large man who walked with no rush in his step. He was deliberate in his motion and as he passed the outer rim of the street light I caught his face. It was Captain Butch.

As he came to the window we locked eyes but didn't acknowledge each other. If he was surprised to see me his face didn't reveal it, instead refocusing his attention on King Tito who rolled down the window.

"How many?" Butch growled.

"Just one this time," Tito said as he grabbed the silver pistol from Alana. He passed it through the opening into Butch's hand. In one quick motion the piece disappeared into one of the Captain's pockets.

"You know where to send the money," Butch said, wrapping his knuckles against the side of the van as he turned and stalked back the way he came. I thought back to all the guns that ended up at the bottom of the ocean from the back of Butch's boat. It was a mental game I played as I tried me to imagine the story that each of them held secret in their barrels and clips. For at least one of those destined to be forgotten to the deep, I knew the whole bloody truth.

Tito stopped the van half a block from my apartment and left the engine running. Neither Alana nor Tito offered a word and I took that as my signal. I opened the door and slid out onto the sidewalk. When I turned to shut the door, Tito was offering a brown cloth bag from an outstretched arm. It was heavy in my hand but feeling the shape inside it was easy to work out what the contents were.

"Just in case," Tito said, turning away from me with both hands on the wheel. I closed the door and the van pulled away from the curb. I watched it turn a corner and disappear.

With what had transpired at The Ukrainian Kitchen and in addition to the gift in the little brown bag, I knew one day the phone would ring or there would be an unexpected knock at the door with a message from King Tito. It was something I was keenly aware of. A favor would be called in and you would feel compelled to make good. Whatever King Tito asked, however difficult or abhorrent, would be done with no questions asked.

. . .

The lights in the taqueria were off. I wasn't sure what time it was but the storefront was usually illuminated well into the early morning hours. There was no one to be seen in the front or the back of the building and as I climbed the back steps I made a pact with myself to find out where Mr. Ortiz was and figure out exactly what had happened. This whole thing was my fault, caused by my greed and fear and I needed to make it right.

The combination of Dr. Walters's pain meds and Boris' body heat were taking their toll as my eyes fluttered and I began to nod off.

A quick jerk of the head from Boris caught my fading attention. His tail began to whip back and forth and then he launched himself from the bed, sliding through the opening of the bedroom door. His claws caught the flesh of my leg as he went airborne. I sat up immediately, my hand massaging the spot where Boris nicked me. That's when I heard the door open.

My heart started racing again and I was sure at this pace of action I would have a heart attack at any moment. I shook as many of the cobwebs as I could from my head and moved from under the sheets and onto the floor. I ran my hand along the dresser top until it found the little brown bag. Inside was a black revolver. I took aim.

The sound of creaking wood as soft footsteps approached and then stopped just outside the bedroom door. I held my breath, finger resting on the trigger.

"Ellis?" Cherry whispered, her voice cutting through the tension like a hot knife through butter. I exhaled and dropped to all fours. The door swung open.

The appearance of me physically when I finally got to my feet must have rocked her because even in the dark shadows the look on her face couldn't be hidden. A half cocked smile crept across my face and I shrugged my shoulders. It is what it is I said without words.

She crossed the room and wrapped her arms around me into a tight embrace. I winced at the constriction and she loosened a bit. I laid my head on her shoulders and the tears came again, falling onto her soft skin that faintly smelled like sun tan lotion.

"Are you okay, baby?"

"I am now," I said, pulling away and wiping the wetness from my eyes. I studied her face. Deep concern mixed with a pinch of pity and a dash of I told you so. It was all there. "Will you stay?"

"Yes. C'mon, let's get you into bed," she said, guiding me until I was lying down under the top sheet. I watched her as she stripped off most of her clothes and climbed in next to me. She always disliked blankets or anything like that and now was no different. She rolled to face me, stroking my face with her hand until the sleep came. I had no fear that night.

CHAPTER TWENTY-THREE

W E   D R A N K   C O F F E E   I N   B E D   A N D   N I B B L E D   O N
leftover, stale tortilla chips. The small porcelain plate sat
between us with microscopic crumbs dotting the crisp white
sheets. The coffee was hot and soothing and the chips helped
with the rumble that had built in my stomach since I awoke. My
body was a house of pain but another dose of painkillers had
started to work their magic.

As we ate I laid out the entire timeline of the previous nights
events. There was always a sense of holding back or keeping
things from Cherry for a variety of reasons but this time I just
let it fly. No detail or action was spared. She was rapt from the
beginning of the tale and when the climax came and Alana
entered the story, Cherry let out an audible gasp. Me too, I
thought to myself. When it was over we sat in silence for a long
while.

"Ortiz is at Harbor Point Memorial. Stable condition but a
pretty nasty cut. Concussion too," she said with a mouthful of
toast.

"How—"

"I saw Mama Inez this morning."

"And?"

"She's okay. Wants to know who's responsible so she can put a curse on them. You gonna go up there?"

"Yes. You?"

"Maybe. I have to go into work for a few hours but if he's still there I will. The way Mama Inez was talking she expected him back on the grill for the dinner rush."

"It wouldn't surprise me. I just feel terrible that he had to pay for something I was mixed up in. I gotta figure a way to make it up to him."

"Maybe it's best if we delay this thing," she said, abruptly changing the course of the conversation.

"Delay?"

"Yeah, I mean, why not? You're pretty fucked up and there's no reason to push it now. If anything the extra time might benefit us."

"I'll be okay."

"Yeah. You always say that but what's the argument for taking the extra time? We could really get it right because frankly, I'm not even sure what the plan is."

I took a deep breath despite the objection from my lungs and ribs and laid it all out for her. What I had going on my end and my expectations to get that damn money out of the ground. As long as the location was accurate I had the team and we were all set. Of course Cherry grunted when Evelyn's name was mentioned but she didn't protest. We're so close I could taste it even over the lingering remnants of blood and coffee swirling around inside of my mouth.

"The board has been cleared for us and to not take advantage of that would be a mistake. Just my opinion but my judgment hasn't exactly been the best the last few weeks so what the fuck do I know."

Cherry reluctantly agreed and we went over the warehouse that had been located and set about securing that space. We set a date and my job would be to contact the rest of the team. Takeoff, Evelyn, Wheels, Cherry and myself would meet once the location was locked down and run through the plan. Then we'd execute it and everyone would be rich. Simple right?

Cherry cleared the dishes and mugs and took them to the kitchen. When she returned she put her clothes on. Her pants were halfway on when she froze at the solid KNOCK KNOCK that came in rapid succession from the back door.

"Cops?" I mouthed at her.

"Sounds like it. You better wobble your ass in there. I'm not here," she said, taking a seat on the edge of the bed as I swung myself out and upright. I threw a t-shirt on to go with my boxer shorts. If it indeed was the coppers at the door I didn't want any questions about the bruising and cigarette burn. It was bad enough that half my face was purple and yellow.

"Good morning. I'm Detective Pryce. This is my partner Detective Chandler. Harbor Point PD. May we come in? Ask you a few questions?" said the curly haired redhead in typical drab detective clothing of gray and more gray. She had a jagged, thin scar under her left eyebrow and when she spoke there was something she was trying to suppress. Deep South twang maybe. Her partner, Chandler, looked like a concrete block in a suit.

I stepped forward and closed the door behind me, joining

them on the porch. I had been around enough cops and detectives to know that you never let them in without a warrant.

"We can talk out here," I said trying to not sound like too much of a dick.

"Fair enough. What happened to your face, Mr. Boone?" She said matter-of-factly.

"Nothing. A little boxing. My reflexes ain't what the used to be."

"I've seen you fight a few times," the human block of granite chimed in.

"You don't say. Is that why you're here? To mock my diminishing skill set?"

"We are looking into the assault on a Mister Gilberto Ortiz. Were you at home last night? See or hear anything out of the ordinary?" she said, watching my face for clues of deception. In reality the only thing racing through my brain was relief that this had nothing to do with three stiffs up in Steelhaven.

"Yeah I just heard about it. The only thing strange is that anyone would want to harm him. Guy is stand up. Everyone likes him," I said as I watched Detective Cinder Block looking through my kitchen window presumably at Boris watching him.

"So that's a no?" Pryce reiterated.

"No what?"

"You didn't hear or see anything?"

"Yeah that's a no."

"Were you home?"

"When?"

"Last night."

"Yes."

"And you didn't see or hear anything out of the ordinary?"

"No."

"You sure about that?" Concrete interjected, turning his attention away from the window and onto me. "Because we talked to Ortiz and he said that there was a similar incident a few days ago involving you."

"You didn't ask me about a few days ago. I can only answer what I'm asked, big guy."

"Smartass," Concrete barked and stepped forward pointing his finger at me. "What really happened to your face?"

Pryce put a restraining hand on her partner's chest in a solid good cop-bad cop move. She put herself between him and me and spoke in a soft voice, "Look, there's been a few shakedowns of local businesses and such over that last few months. Protection rackets. Threats. We don't want that to happen here so if you could help us out we'd be grateful. I need you to tell us what happened to you."

"A couple of days back I came home late and there were a few guys in the alley where I usually park. I told them to move and they didn't want to so it got a little rough. I have a tendency to run my mouth so it was mostly my fault. You're talkin' mob shit. Extortion. This was not that. Just a dust up over a parking spot."

"A parking spot?" Concrete said again.

"That's it. That's all I got for you guys."

"What'd they look like?" Pryce asked with a hint of annoyance to her voice.

"It was dark. One guy was short, one was tall. I don't know I didn't get a good look at them."

"Why didn't you report it?"

"Is that a serious question?" I said with half a laugh.

"C'mon, Pryce, let's go. This guy is fucking worthless." Concrete said and put a hand on Pryce's shoulder.

She dug into her jacket pocket and produced a standard white business card and passed it to me. "You change your mind or you need anything you give us a call, okay?"

They turned and went down the steps but not before Detective Concrete threw me a menacing glance, a real I-know-who-the-fuck-you-are look. The card was standard with the Harbor Point PD logo and a slogan about protecting and serving or something. Dead center it read: MORGAN PRYCE - SPECIAL INVESTIGATIONS DIVISION. I had a thought that I'd be seeing her again.

I watched them walk across the parking lot and I heard her say, "Of course I don't believe him."

CHAPTER TWENTY-FOUR

AFTER THE POLICE LEFT MY APARTMENT I MADE MY
way over to the hospital to visit with Mr. Ortiz. His spirits were
high and we laughed as we shared an ice cream cup from the
cafeteria. He asked about my visible injuries and I promised him
I would tell him one day.

Cherry had secured the warehouse we would be using for a
base of operations. It was located way beyond The Bottoms in
an area that, not too long ago, was a haven for the homeless and
drug addicted. A tent city had sprouted up and it was a very
dangerous place for a number of years. At some point a
commercial developer came in, demolished the makeshift town
and built a maze like industrial park. It was perfect.

Gathering the team was a bit like herding cats but eventually
a day and time were agreed upon to meet and do a rundown of
the plan in general.

The only hiccup and it really wasn't that, was when I was
leaving the apartment early in the week. I pulled out onto the
street that ran in front of the taqueria and to my left, seated at a
table at the front of the restaurant, was Detective Morgan Price.

She didn't see me as she was engaged in a hot plate of something. Coincidence? Maybe but she struck me as the kind of thorn you didn't want in your side for very long.

As I tried to push thoughts of the ginger detective from my mind I spotted a grayish blue sedan pull into the lot behind me. He was late but this was not out of the ordinary and I had become accustomed to it. The sedan reversed its course and backed in next to me so each car's driver side were directly opposed to each other.

The tinted window methodically descended and there he was: Landry Hampton III. A portly man who always managed to have a stain on his wrinkled dress shirt. Landry had been in my employ, or rather my debt, for two and half years and it was grating on him. He was more and more agitated each time we would meet.

"I think this should square us," he said like he always did, extending his chubby arm out from his window toward mine. I reached out and took the small manila envelope he was waving at me. I smiled at him.

"Nice to see you too, Landry."

"Fuck you, Ellis. I told you the last time that was the last time. We're evened up. Don't call me no more. I'm serious."

"We're evened up when I say we are. Don't turn your phone off."

"Eat shit."

The sedan jerked forward and sped off leaving a cloud of tan dust in its wake. I laughed to myself as I opened up the envelope and checked the contents. As always, Landry had delivered even though it ate his insides to do so. Inside was an official document from the county Department of Health & Human Services. The final piece we needed to move forward. It was nice to have friends, however reluctant, inside the marbled confines of City Hall.

I headed downtown as the sun was just dipping below the horizon, casting a pastel hue over the city. The route I chose was not one I would normally travel at this time of day during the ramp up to beach season. The Cutlass crawled along Atlantic Avenue in step with the throngs of cars and pedestrians. It was a cool night and the amusements would be in full swing well into the evening.

Sometimes I did this and I didn't know why. I would roll down the window and let what Harbor Point was supposed to be about wash over me as I drove. The smells of food and screams of delight coupled with the easy breeze from the ocean were soothing somehow, for both body and soul so I could deal with a little traffic. It was a fair trade.

I moved out of the Atlantic Circle, through The Bottoms and out into the marshlands. It was quiet and much darker than the rest of the city that lay behind me and I wondered, given Harbor Point's flirtation with organized crime in the past, how many bodies found their end in this waterlogged and barren stretch of land.

The giant compound of the industrial park would be hard to miss once the sun went down if you didn't know where you were going. Even during business hours the massive corporate spread seemed to be operating at a little less than half capacity. Cherry nailed the location on this one.

She was leaning in the doorway as I pulled up close and put the car in park and turned the ignition. Evelyn's car was parked against a chain link fence and that explained the rather sour look spread across Cherry's face. It was nothing specific, those two just didn't mix.

"There wasn't someone else—"

"Stop. I trust her and there are very few of those options floating around at the moment. You're just gonna have to learn how to play nice together for the next couple of days. You think you can manage that?" I said as I walked to the doorway. Fine, she didn't like her but I wasn't in the mood for her child like complaints. We had a job to do.

Cherry and I entered the building and it seemed there were some remains from a previous business strewn about. Boxes and some chairs occupied an office area with a large door at the back.

"How'd you find this place?" I asked.

"One of our competitors uses a place around the corner for casket storage. I put it on the company account."

"You think that's a good idea?"

"Why wouldn't it be?"

"Meyer. Can't imagine she would be too keen on the idea of paying for a place she wasn't using. Might bring questions you don't want." Cherry fidgeted and broke eye contact at the mention of Cathy Meyer.

"Let me handle that. Besides, even if she does find out I'll be long gone by then," she said, picking at the corner of her thumb with the forefinger. She did this when she was nervous or lying or both. Cherry was a terrible card player.

"So that's it then. We make the score and you blow? Seems about right."

"I was gonna tell you but I figured you'd have something shitty to say so..." she trailed off.

We entered the warehouse, passed a garage bay for several

vehicles then turned a corner into a cavernous space with steel racks attached to walls for stacking. At a cheap makeshift table sat Takeoff, Wheels and Evelyn, who looked at me with annoyance as she ran a file along her long green fingernails. Takeoff had a pair of headphones on that he removed when he saw me and Wheels looked like he might have been asleep. I clapped my hands and his eyes snapped open.

"I know it's unusual but we're going to lay it out and then if you wanna walk you can walk but from the jump I'm just going to say three words. Twenty. Million. Dollars. I paused, "Those looks tell me we can proceed," I said, my voice echoing off the concrete walls.

Wheels had pulled his massive body up from a slouched position, now focused and attentive. If Takeoff had a pen and paper he would have been ready to take notes and Evelyn sat frozen, the file still resting against her fingernail. The scowl on her face had softened significantly.

I waved my arm in Cherry's direction and she took over. From the corner she lifted and plopped a big cardboard box down on the table in front of them. Inside were plastic wrapped uniforms of brown and tan that she extracted and handed out.

"Before we leave tonight you need to try these on," she said as each of them inspected the package they had been given. Cherry continued, breaking down the cemetery location and the inherent difficulty of getting a coffin out of the ground in broad daylight. She turned back to me.

"Any questions before I dig into the finer points?" I asked. Evelyn's hand shot up. "This ain't school. Shout 'em out if you got 'em."

"Who we rippin' off?" Evelyn asked.

"No one that's around anymore to care about it," I said.

"Dead or not around. There's a difference."

"I'll put it this way. The only people alive that know about that cash are in this room," Cherry said from over my shoulder. My mind flashed back to the basement at the Ukrainian Kitchen.

"So here's how it's gonna go down," I began, taking a seat at the table, "in two days time me and Takeoff will get the backhoe from his old man's place and drive it out to Steelhaven. Wheels and Evelyn, you will meet here and pick up a van that will be waiting and meet us out at the cemetery. Cherry will coordinate with you here. She's gonna hold back because she works across the street and has a lot of dealings with this place. We don't wanna draw any unnecessary attention. We dig, we lift and we get the hell out of there. Wheels and Evelyn will travel with the cargo while me and Takeoff drop the backhoe. We'll rendezvous here when it's done."

Silence.

"Shiiiit. Why in the fuck would they let us roll up in there and just yank a fuckin' casket out the ground? I mean I want that cash as much as the rest of you cats but ain't no way in hell they just gonna let us dig it up," Wheels protested, tipping his chair back on two legs. He rubbed his forehead with his massive hand, trying to make sense of it.

"They will have no choice," I said calmly.

"And why the fuck not?"

"Because it's all legal and on the level," I said, pulling the manila envelope from my jacket pocket. The letter inside was creased in thirds and I unfolded it slowly and slid it across the table to Wheels. Takeoff and Evelyn leaned in and examined the paper over his shoulder. I looked back and winked at Cherry.

Wheels laughed and tossed the paper back to me. "You a

slick ass mothafucka Boone. I see you. What about firepower? What we rollin' with?"

"Nothing. No guns, pure deception. That's what the uniforms and that piece of paper are for," I said. I got up from the table and joined Cherry, who was standing a few feet away from the group. "If there are no more questions then get to trying on those uniforms and I'll see you in a few days."

The cigarette smoke didn't feel great in my lungs but when Cherry passed it to me it felt like the right thing to do. It was almost pitch black in the parking lot and as we watched Evelyn's red tail lights pull away and fade into the distance Cherry finally spoke, "That went okay, yeah?"

"Yeah they're good. Where's your head at?"

"The truth?"

"The fact that you have to ask me that is a problem. Yeah the fuckin' truth."

"I feel like I'm gonna throw up."

"Me too."

She moved close and wrapped her arm around my waist and whispered, "I think it's gonna go off just the way it's supposed to."

CHAPTER TWENTY-FIVE

IT'S A SLOW BUILD BUT THE NERVES DON'T HIT YOU right away. First there's the arrival at the venue. You're cool, relaxed and ready to go. As the day wears on there's some last minute interviews to take care of, medicals and pre-fight meetings. Once the trunks go on and your trainer starts to wrap your hands you start to feel it, faint at first but the ramp up is quick. Next thing you know you're hitting the mitts and bouncing around to build up a lather. Then the word comes that's it's go time and as you maneuver the tunnel or backstage area the distant rumble of the crowd hits you and every hair on your body stands at attention. Now the adrenaline is coursing through you and exists as a separate entity, fueling you forward. It's a propellant that will push you for however long you last. Finally, it's just a curtain between you and immortality and you can't wait. You live and breathe this kind of intense pressure. That feeling cannot be duplicated. Or so I thought.

I sat in the cab of a long hauler with Takeoff behind the wheel. There was that familiar rumble in my guts. The only discernible difference was that I had a gun in my coat and wasn't going somewhere to get my brains beat in.

The imitation Sheriff's uniforms that Cherry procured fit well enough but all, at least mine and Takeoff's, were a little short. The pants sat at least three or four inches above the ankle. It was comical.

Takeoff said nothing the entire drive out to Steelhaven. He was focused on the road, constantly checking the rear and side view mirrors. The mini backhoe that was loaded onto the hauler was plenty big enough to move some dirt around and small enough to not draw too much wandering eye traffic. It took thirty minutes before Takeoff guided us toward the exit for Steelhaven.

"Pull it over right here," I instructed as Takeoff brought the truck and trailer to rest against the curb. We were up the street from the main entrance to the cemetery and I could see that just outside the fence was the long white cargo van emblazoned with the Coastal County seal on the door. "Just chill and I'll signal you when to bring it in."

"Ten four," Takeoff said, skulking down in his seat and throwing on a large pair of sunglasses. Between the two of us he definitely looked more like a cop.

I was sweating under the polyester uniform as I crossed the road and covered the hundred or so yards to the main gate opening. Through the fence were row after row of headstones with a smattering of flower arrangements and American flags.

"Morning baby. You ready to get this money?" Evelyn said with a smile. I rested an elbow inside the open window and gave her a wink. Wheels flashed a peace sign into the air.

From my jacket I pulled the manila envelope and passed it to Evelyn and said, "Here you go."

"Thanks for letting me be the one to do it," she said, smiling wider.

"You got it down? What to say?"

"This is an Exhumation Order from the Department of Health. Coastal County Sheriff's Department blah, blah, blah. I got it."

"Okay. You ready, Wheels?" I asked, ignoring the fact that Evelyn was going to wing the whole thing. Fuck it. I figured she had probably seen enough episodes of Law & Order to survive. Besides, there was no one here in a position to know better.

"Ready, son," he growled, navigating the gear shift into place and pulling the van under the wrought iron over hang and onto the grounds. I followed a few paces behind keeping an eye out for anything suspicious, besides us of course.

We entered the main building in lock step. It was small, old and cluttered. The entire structure seemed to house just one room that served as both a waiting area and office.

Behind a desk in the corner sat an elderly man reading a dusty old paperback. He rocked slowly back and forth in a swivel chair underneath a ceiling fan that was wobbling at dangerous angles.

"Excuse me, sir," Evelyn called out. No response as the old man kept rocking back and forth, focused on his book. I nudged her with my shoulder and she shuffled up to the desk. It appeared as if he didn't know she was there until she shot out a hand and snapped her fingers.

"Whatcha got for me?" he said with a throat seemingly full of gravel.

Evelyn placed the official order in his wrinkled hand. He read through it, mumbling to himself the whole way.

"Okay, okay, shouldn't be a problem here. See this kinda thing all the time. Well not all the time but you know what I mean now. Just need the old John Hancock on...now where is that god damn form? I swear people be touchin' my shit. Oh, here it is right under my god damn nose," he said, finally turning to face Evelyn. I saw her back tense up as Curtis, indicated by a patch above his left breast, went wide eyed.

"Cocoa? Cocoa Brown! Hot damn that is you. Girl, I ain't seen you in about a minute," Curtis exclaimed, slapping a hand on his knee. Evelyn shot me a look and I took a step toward them. Curtis' brain seemed to catch up. "Now what's all this here with the po-lice getup?"

Evelyn didn't respond. Instead she started to back away from old Curtis but he took two steps in her direction and said, "Shit, is this one of those things were you pretend to be police and then start dancin' around nekkid? It ain't even my birthday. Did Muncey put you up to this? That ol' son of a bitch."

Evelyn was still backing up with Curtis stalking her and I had had enough. I pulled the gun from my pocket and had it trained on the old man before he saw it and he damn near walked into the barrel.

"Sit down old man," I said and waited til he realized what was happening and sat down into the creaky chair.

Wheels came up next to me and asked, "I thought you said no guns?"

"No guns for you. Now Curtis listen to me very carefully. Just sit there and behave yourself and you won't get hurt and we'll be out of here in no time. Do you understand me?" I said clearly. I wanted to make sure this old bird was getting the message.

"I understand that this some bullshit. Cocoa what's goin' on baby? What you wanna do old Curtis like this for. I tip you fine, don't I?" he pleaded.

"Of course, Curtis, baby. This ain't got nothin' to do with you. Just let us do our thing and we'll be outta your hair," she said in a smooth and seductive tone.

Curtis mulled over the words and had some terms of his own. "Y'all can do whatever you want but next time I come down to The Cheetah there better be some extra sugar waitin' for me, ya hear?"

"I'll have some extra sugar for you. I promise."

"Okay, then. Do what you gotta do and get the fuck outta here. And don't say nothin' cause I don't wanna know nothin' about nothin'"

Evelyn turned to me and looked like she could tear my skin off. "What the fuck?" she said through gritted teeth.

"What? How was I supposed to know you knew the guardsman intimately? Look forget it. We have to move. We're already running behind."

"We'll talk about this later. Believe you me," she said with anger still hot in her voice.

I smiled and handed her the gun. "Keep an eye on the old guy. Maybe you two can catch up," I said with a laugh as I grabbed Wheels by the arm and led him outside. I'd pay for that one later. Just before I made it out the door I could hear Curtis whistle and say, "You still got it girl. Git yo fine ass over here."

The gravesite that Cherry had given us was unkempt compared

to the surrounding plots. No flowers, it was overgrown and the headstone looked as if it had never been cleaned. This was a good sign and took some of the edge off because up until this point it was simply assumed on my part that there definitely wasn't a body in the coffin we were about to dig up. Now that I stood over the grave, my hands were a little clammy at the task that stood before us.

Takeoff had maneuvered the hauler carefully through the narrow gates and stopped on the service road that ran along the cemetery's edge. There wasn't much ground to cover once he was behind the controls of the backhoe and easily navigated to the site. Now, with the bucket poised in the air, ready to rip through the earth, we were ready to go. I gave him a quick nod and Takeoff did the rest.

As the pile of dirt and mud got bigger Wheels leaned against the van and smoked cigarettes and gave the illusion that he was playing the part of lookout. What did I care? He wasn't there for anything other than to drive and if need be drive fast.

I did my best to keep my mind off of Vivian Marie Swanson, loving mother who devoted her life to charity. At least that's what was chiseled into the massive stone monument. The questions came fast. How did she die? According to the market she was only sixty years old. Cancer probably. It's always cancer. And if she was a devoted mother why had the site been so neglected? I imagined the children moved away after she died. Ultimately the answer I wanted most was what actually became of Vivian's remains? Did Kramer just ship them off to the crematorium without a thought? I'm glad that guy was dead.

My eyes swept the surrounding area. It was eerily quiet and empty but that was probably just my anxiety starting to kick up. Then, very quickly, I felt the sensation that someone was watching us. I turned and from down the hill, barely visible was a small figure in the parking lot of the funeral home. I cupped my hand over my eyes and squinted trying to get a better look. Was that Ms. Meyer? A moment passed and the person was off, walking rapidly to a car. They got in a peeled out of the parking lot, kicking up a massive amount of gravel dust. I watched as the vehicle picked up speed and disappeared.

The bucket on the backhoe hit something with a crunching sound and snapped me out it. Takeoff raised the arm and hopped down from his seat. Wheels heard it too and he wobbled over. The three of us peered down into the open earth and saw the cherry wood top of the casket. We said nothing.

After our little moment I cracked at Wheels. "Get the crowbar." He quick stepped it to the van and returned with the hard iron stick in his hand. He tossed it to me and I jumped down into the hole. There was very little room to work so I asked Takeoff to give me some more space along the side to get my arms moving.

It was not easy getting that damn thing open but once I felt it give I hesitated before popping it completely.

"What you waiting for?" Wheels said from above.

"You wanna do it?" I said.

He shook his head back and forth, his jowls wiggling.

I took a deep breath and lifted, popping the lid. Without realizing it I had closed my eyes.

"Open your eyes, Ellis," Takeoff said, the pitch in in his voice elevated.

Four large black duffel bags were packed tightly against the white satin of the interior. My heart began to thump very loudly in my ears and my hand trembled as it gripped one of the zippers and pulled.

Inside were a series of vacuum sealed packages stuffed with hundred dollar bills.

"Back the van up," I said to Wheels, who took off running, "and when I get out of this hole, start filling it in." That sent Takeoff back to his perch on the backhoe.

We quickly loaded the bags into the back of the van and while Takeoff did cleanup duty we went to pick up Evelyn from the main guardhouse.

Wheels pulled up to the door and we both went inside but not before I took out a small knife and cut one of the sealed packs of cash open and grabbed a stack of bills. When we got inside we heard a giddy laughter from Curtis and Evelyn threatening to shoot his old ass.

Her face changed when I tossed a wink her way and she knew we were good. I handed Curtis the stack of money and we left before he could react at the amount. That should keep him from yapping to anybody important or dangerous.

Before Evelyn jumped in the van she handed my gun to me but I pushed it back toward her. "Hold onto it for a little while," I said, nodding my head in Wheels direction. "Keep an eye on him. He gets out of line, remind him of where he stands. I'll see you in about an hour." I leaned in and kissed her on the cheek.

It took some time to get the backhoe loaded and by the time we got on the highway back to Harbor Point the van was no where to be seen. This was something I wrestled with the entire planning phase. Should I ride with the money? Was it a colossal, with a capital C, mistake to let it out of my sight? The answer was two fold. First, I trusted Evelyn with my life so I knew she'd do right by me. There was also an aspect of self-preservation to it. I couldn't gauge Cherry's honesty about whether or not anyone else knew about all of it and would be looking for the money. So it was selfish on my part and I didn't feel great about it.

When we had returned the hauler and backhoe and got in the Cutlass I had chewed my fingers til blood trickled from the skin.

CHAPTER TWENTY-SIX

Something was wrong. Pain instantly surged across my head and the blood began to pound in all areas of my body. The aching in my ribs, which had since been manageable, flared causing me to wince.

"You have a weapon on you?" I asked Takeoff with urgency.

"No," he replied, not sounding confident that he understood what was happening.

A few clues. Cherry's car was not in the lot and one of the garage bays was wide open. The van faced out with one of the side doors ajar. This was too sloppy and Evelyn, let alone Cherry, would not allow this. Wheels maybe. Fucking Wheels. Could that oaf throw down a double cross and have me miss it completely?

I had my answer as I crept through the door to the office, Takeoff following with cautious steps. Wheels was laid out on the floor face down. Blood was running from his head as well as at least one bullet hole in his thigh. The carpet under his massive body had turned an ugly shade of brownish red.

I stepped over his body and moved slowly to the van. A

cursory look inside confirmed what I already knew: the money bags were gone. The only word that my brain would allow was fuck. Over and over again as we moved to the center of the warehouse I said that word.

It was empty and I was about to completely lose it when Takeoff whacked my arm with his hand. "There," he said, pointing to the floor by the table that sat in the center of the room. A collection of blood droplets ran away from the table and turned into a smear across the drab, gray concrete.

At the end of the trail, under a mound of boxes and a roll of bubble wrap, was Evelyn. Her hands were bound behind her and a rag was stuffed in her mouth. Just above the elbow ran a five inch gash that was leaking blood. It wasn't bad but it wasn't nothing either. Her face turned to rage when she saw us and the words, inaudible because of the gag, came fast and furious.

Takeoff disappeared and returned with a box cutter just as I was yanking the obstruction from her mouth.

"That bitch! I swear to god Ima kill her Ellis and then Ima kill yo dumbass," she said with vitriol. I cut her loose and she got to her feet.

"Wait a god damn second. Cherry did this? What happened?" I pleaded.

"We got fucking ambushed man. Never had a fucking chance."

I grabbed her by the shoulders and squared her up so I could look into her eyes. "Tell me exactly what happened."

"Whatchu mean? We got here and they was waiting for us. Tied me up and Wheels tried to fight and make a break for it."

"They?"

"Yeah Cherry and that crazy fuck Buckshot."

"Sonofabitch."

I rubbed my face harder than necessary and spots developed momentarily in my vision. It was like a bad fucking dream. Stupid, stupid, stupid. I was falling through a tunnel inside my own mind until Evelyn snapped me out of it. "What the fuck are we gonna do, Ellis?" she yelled.

I tried to focus my thoughts but the only thing that came was that I was going to kill Cherry and her uncle, with my bare hands if need be.

"Okay, okay…Takeoff, go check on Wheels," I barked and Takeoff disappeared into the front office. I turned my attention to Evelyn and said, "Where's my gun?"

"Where you think it is, genius? They took it."

"How long ago did they peel outta here?"

"Twenty minutes. Thirty tops."

"Come on."

We ran to the garage bays and met with Takeoff who shook his head letting us know Wheels was no longer a part of the team. It was a shame. I thought I had gotten him killed once before but now it was a reality. I'd deal with that one later.

The van luckily still had the keys in the ignition. "Evelyn, take the van and go to The Bottoms. If you see these pricks prowling around anywhere you call me. Do not do anything stupid. Not without me at least. You," I said with a finger pointed at Takeoff, "go with her and do exactly what she says." He nodded and went to the passenger side and climbed in.

"What're you gonna do?"

"I don't know," I said as I took Evelyn's face in my hands. "I'm sorry."

"Fuck you, Ellis. Man up and let's go get our money back."

• • •

The van swerved as it raced from the warehouse lot. I sat behind the wheel, my hands and knuckles were sore from pounding the steering wheel a few times. It wasn't fair to the Cutlass. She didn't do anything but hey, you hurt the ones you love right?

My thigh began to vibrate. It couldn't be Evelyn. She wouldn't even be through the marshes yet. Maybe it was Judas herself I thought as I fished the phone from my pocket.

The display screen indicated it was CAPTAIN BUTCH. My finger rubbed the button to silence along the side but at the last second flipped the phone open and pressed it to my ear.

"Not a great time Butch. What's up?" I barked.

"I'll make it quick then. You remember when you told me to call if I ever saw your girl down here again?"

"Yeah"

"Well this is that call."

"When?"

"Now. I can see her."

"Is she alone?"

"No."

I flipped the phone closed and dropped it onto the floor. It would take thirty minutes to get to the marina with lights and traffic.

CHAPTER TWENTY-SEVEN

THE CUTLASS ROCKED UP AND DOWN WITH A VIOLENT motion as I took the corner too short into the lot across from the Marina. My foot jammed the brake pedal almost to the floor causing rocks and dirt to spray in all directions. I was out of the car and across the street in a blur.

I caught Butch's large frame hunched over sitting on the back of his boat smoking a cigar. He stood tall when he saw me approaching and didn't wait for me to ask. "Down there," he pointed to the far end of the dock, where it curved outward from the land and jutted into the water. "What do you need me to do?"

"Just keep an eye out," I said, passing him without stopping. My legs quickened their pace and the boards creaked under the rapid thud of my feet.

Then I saw her. It was a brief glimpse through the forest of bobbing boats but that it was Cherry was unmistakable. She had stepped up briefly, as if standing on something, but disappeared into the interior of the boat she was on. That boat was now pulling away from the dock. I took off at a dead run, following the curved angle of the dock to the boat's launch point.

It was a sleek looking vessel, white and about thirty feet in length. At the center, shaped like a box, was a glass enclosure that housed the captain's area and the entrance to the cabin below. There was no one visible on deck and all I could see through the glass was a blurry figure guiding the boat out to sea.

The distance was too far to make a clean jump to the boat but as I launched myself into the air I aimed for the starboard side where a thick piece of nylon rope hung low, almost touching the surface.

The water was cold and as I broke the surface my arm extended and stretched, searching for a grip on the rope. The tips of my fingers found, slipped away and ultimately landed their mark, curling around the line. I flexed my bicep and pulled my body through the green, murky water and gripped the rope with my other hand. I held on with an iron grip as the boat yanked me out to sea with it. The water cascaded all around me, filling my ears, nose and mouth. The saltwater was rancid against my tongue and I struggled against the instinct to choke and cough which would only open the floodgates. I clamped my jaw and held my breath only sucking in air when I could.

The engines kicked into a higher gear sending a harsh vibration through my body that now banged against the side with a more violent frequency. I looked around and saw nothing except sky and water. My mind told my hands to let go and swim back to shore. Was anything on this boat worth my life?

My share of twenty million reasons jolted through me. And it was literally slipping through my fingers. It wasn't just about the money either. The girl. It always circled back to that damn girl. She operated in ways that I could never understand and yet she laid down real estate in my psyche that I feared could never be scrubbed clean. She walked away from me once without a word and I couldn't, for my own sanity, let that happen again.

The rage bubbled and reinvigorated the muscles in my arm. Going hand over hand, with each tendon and muscle stretched to its limit, I managed to throw an arm over the edge followed by a leg and hoisted my self on to the deck. It sounded like a water balloon exploding when I landed, water logged and gasping for breath.

I half expected a welcoming party but as I laid there, motionless and freezing, there was nothing but the whipping wind of the ocean air. I pulled myself into a crouch and surveyed the deck while the engines roared beneath the polished mahogany wood.

Positioned behind the glass enclosure, at the rear of the boat, I could see straight through to the wide open expanse of water. A cursory glance over my shoulder revealed the same thing: nothing.

There was a slim figure at the captain's controls, solitary and stiff. Immediately to the left of where the Captain stood was an opening that presumably led to quarters below deck. That's where Cherry and Buckshot would be with my money. I scanned the area for a makeshift weapon of any kind because despite my primal desire to kill both of them, it wasn't going to be easy empty handed. I found nothing of consequence and found myself anchored to the spot I was crouched in, unsure of the next move.

Again, I glanced back over my shoulder as the thought of death entered my mind. A few small dots on the horizon now and what looked to be a commercial fishing boat heading toward shore. The wind picked up and caused a loud whistling in my ears and my shirt to flap rapidly against my skin.

Resigned to the only option I stood, steadied myself against the sway and approached the cabin, my eyes fixed on the angular man steering the ship. The wet soles of my sneakers squeaked along the deck and when I reached the door I turned the lever quickly and slipped inside.

The air conditioner turned my skin to gooseflesh and my teeth instantly began to chatter. There was no reaction from the man standing about five feet from me. When the boat hit a swell the door behind me closed with a loud popping sound.

"Do you fancy yourself a cowboy, Ellis Boone?" the captain said. It wasn't a male voice but the smooth, focused and soft tone of a woman. That voice strung a familiar chord. "Play cowboys and Indians when you were a child?"

She turned and stared a hole through me. It was that peckish woman Cathy Meyer. Instinctively I took a step backward and bumped the glass wall.

"I must assume you always chose the role of the Indian, yes? Because you do not know when to accept defeat." She continued with slow, monotone syllables falling from her mouth. "It could be taken as a character defect in many circles but I view it as a positive. I admire the moxie. One must be careful though in all their actions because much like a fly many forces will conspire to swat you dead."

I regained my footing and took back the ground I had given up. "Same could be said for stealing a man's money."

She took her hands from the wheel and spun full around to me. A dry rhythmic cackle shot from her lungs and she said, "Foolish boy. That money is and always was mine. You were simply blinded by your own greed and lust to see it."

The small door at the bottom of the steps opened with a creak, the hinges screaming at each other. The long barrel of a shotgun came into view first, followed by the heavily muscled arms of its owner Buckshot. I hadn't laid eyes on Buckshot in a long time but he looked more grizzled and nasty than I remembered, if that was possible.

He moved methodically until we were on even ground, his steel tube of death trained on me. "Shoulda kept those feet on dry land, Ellis."

"Me? I kinda pegged you for a land lover myself," I said with faux cockiness in my words.

"Yeah well shit ain't always what it seems. You feel me?" he said with a smile.

From below Cherry emerged, my stolen gun in her hand. "Yeah I feel you," I said. The words came out dry and hollow. Cherry's eyes were on mine. There was no hate or vitriol in her gaze though and I had to wonder how much of this had been her idea. Again, the justification came to me without being able to stop it. I shook it away and wondered how it was all going to end.

I left the shotgun and turned my attention back to Meyer. "Help me get this...whatever this is. You get me to dig up the money just to what? Split with it? That can't be all there is. You could've done this shit yourself."

Meyer looked to Cherry who smirked and shrugged her shoulders. "I knew you would do it if I asked." If not for the prospect of a softball sized hole in my chest I would have crossed the room and hit her.

"You used me just so you could stick the god damn knife in my back? That can't be it? Can't be. We are in the middle of the fucking ocean Cherry just give it to me straight. For once in your miserable fucking life be honest with me." On the word miserable Buckshot pumped the shotgun and shuffled forward a half step, a lifetime of violence in his eyes.

Meyer gave her a nod. She stepped in my direction and her face softened. "You could come with us. We could use someone like you, Ellis."

I did not possess the mental capacity to process a response like that coming from her. She was always working some angle and looking to game the system. Was this an evolution of that? It all sounded off the rails to me and it was a scary proposition when Ellis Boone was the most logical person in the room.

She opened her arms and moved a bit closer with her pitch. "It's something good I promise. It's worthy. It'd be a real opportunity for you to do something with your life instead of...I don't know. Doing what you do."

"A good cause? Life purpose? What the fuck are you talking about, Cherry?" I laughed hard. It was an uncontrollable reaction. "People are dead. You know that right? You killed one of my guys. And what about Kramer? Lemme guess, that was you self-righteous pricks too. A sacrifice for your bullshit cause."

Buckshot's finger slid from a position just above the trigger to resting directly on the kill switch.

"My late husband was a psychopath who tried to end my life to protect himself so no, not for the cause, but because he had to die. There was no other way for him," Meyer said.

"Your handiwork I assume," I said to Buckshot.

"I got some people on the inside. I was gonna handle his little henchman too but somebody beat me to it."

Any hope or chance that I clung to of getting off the boat with the money had abandoned ship along with most of my confidence that I would leave with my life. I could not listen or deal with these fucking people any longer. Whatever her deal was, brainwashed or not, Cherry had gone to a place that I could not join.

"So what now? I say no and you dump me in the ocean?" I asked to anyone who would answer.

Buckshot obliged me. "Pretty much."

"Don't say no. Come with us," Cherry implored again.

The ramifications of a negative answer washed over me. Buckshot clearly had no problem with that outcome, even Meyer. Would Cherry actually let them gun me down in cold blood? I wasn't so sure and my heart began to race.

"If I say yes how are you ever gonna be sure that I'm in it with you all the way? Whatever delusional shit's going on between the three of you I don't want any part of and you all know that from the jump. So if I say yes, I'll be waiting for that bullet in that back of my head since you'd be wondering the same thing. Questioning my commitment and waiting for a reason to plug me."

"The answer is no then?" Meyer said with the intonation of a statement and not so much a question.

I said nothing. My eyes stared at Cherry, trying to burn a hole through her soul if she still had one.

"Outside," commanded Buckshot.

Out on the deck the temperature had dropped significantly with the swift wind picking up seawater and depositing it as a spray over the deck. Buckshot and Cherry had followed me out but Meyer remained inside, commanding the boat through the choppy waves.

My eyes swept across the vast expanse of the greenish black water and I knew, one way or another, that I was going in.

Whether it was of my own doing or at the insistence of a shotgun shell had yet to be determined. The idea of jumping came to me just as Buckshot pressed the barrel against my back, essentially erasing any chance I had of making it to the water without being blasted.

In the distance a twinkle caught my eye. It was a reflection of some sort and I was grateful for it. It could have been a boat or a piece of trash but I concentrated on it hard, waiting for the Angel of Death to process my paperwork. I thought of my father but couldn't quite get a mental grasp on his face. The only image that came to me was when he was at the end and he looked thirty years older than he was.

I could hear Cherry talking behind me but the sound was faded and distant. The words came but they were incomprehensible to me, the world around me had slowed to a crawl. The gun nudged me hard in the back as everything caught back up with itself in real time.

"Ellis!" Cherry shouted over the gusting wind. I turned and looked her directly in the eyes. They were twinkling and full of selfishness and regret. Before closing them she mouthed the words: I'm sorry.

Buckshot jerked and twisted the gun barrel away from my body and rammed, with the full force of a hurricane, the solid wood handle against my temple.

My knees buckled and I stumbled backwards, crashing into the edge of the boat. I was in trouble and hurt badly only this time there was no referee to step in. No trainer to throw in the towel and save me.

Buckshot placed a palm on my chest and shoved. The distance between going over the side and crashing into the water could've taken five seconds or five years. I was out when I hit the water but the piercing cold temperature served as a natural defibrillator and jolted me back to consciousness.

With my arms and legs in sync I propelled myself to the surface. I twisted in all directions. No sign of the boat. No sign of anything. Bobbing up and down the waves took me where they wanted. I didn't put up a fight.

My head throbbed and bled profusely. The slick blood poured down my face and mixed with the ocean water all around me. A heaviness began to creep in followed by an overwhelming urge to sleep.

I rubbed the droplets of water and blood from my eyes and did one more cursory look around. It was useless. Even if I guessed the correct direction I could never hope to swim the distance.

Time spent above the water became less and my legs lacked the energy to move at the pace required. More and more water found its way into my mouth no matter how hard I pressed my lips together. I was a sinking ship whose crew desperately tried to plug the leaks and stem the tide of inevitability.

Inhaling deeply I sunk below the surface once more in an effort to give my limbs a rest from the battle against the waves. The dim light of the overcast sky above offered the only illumination against the perpetual blackness below. I kicked hard in attempt to make it back to the surface but there wasn't enough force behind it. I hung there in the water in a state of suspended animation. The world slowed and ground to a halt as air left my lungs and was replaced by water. I thought of my father again but this time as a young and vibrant man, beaming down at me with that gap toothed smile. Serene calm flooded my senses and a peace that I had never felt overcame me.

A dark shadow cut through the fading light from above and

low rumble sent vibrations through the water, momentarily interrupting my moment of enlightenment. A sharp pain dug at my armpit and the light came rushing toward me. It grew brighter and brighter until I crashed through the surface, oxygen filling my lungs. I coughed and water spewed from my mouth. I looked skyward and saw a face, old and weathered, flashing a gap toothed grin.

"Not today ace," said the voice. A large hand reached out to me and I reached back but either out of sheer exhaustion or shock, the blackness forming in my head overtook me and I passed out.

CHAPTER TWENTY-EIGHT

IT HAD BEEN THREE WEEKS SINCE MY BODY WAS fished out of the ocean like a marlin or tuna and the nightmares hadn't stopped. I had been over to Dr. Walter's place and she recommended a good shrink but I didn't think I was ready to have someone crack open my head and go digging.

The face of the late Frank Boone had come to my dreams, uninvited, on a regular basis when I attempted sleep. Only, it wasn't the ghost of my father who magically pulled me from the jaws of death but Captain Butch who, as he tells it, had set off just after we pulled out of the marina and kept his distance best he could. From a set of binoculars he saw me go in and sprung into action.

"Shoulda played the lottery that day. A hundred to one shot that I found yer ass," he said to me over beers a few days later. "I'm not sayin' I'm ever gonna come collect, cause that ain't the type of fella I am, but you owe me one, kid."

I woke up hours later on Butch's boat, my clothes stripped off and a mountain of blankets piled on top of me. That old buzzard stayed with me all night with the right concoction of teas, booze and food and by the next morning I was able to get home on my own. Again, before I left the marina, Butch reminded me of the debt.

He was right. I owed him my life and I put that one in the column of unconditional favors I had outstanding. Far too many by my count but without them it wouldn't really matter would it?

I got in my car and finally had a look at my face and the place where Buckshot had tried to separate my head from my neck. It was bad but my face was getting accustomed to taking a beating. I left the marina and went straight home. Boris's meows did my perpetual headache no favors but after he was fed we curled up in bed and slept for what felt like a week. He didn't leave my side and his constant purring and warm body helped me stay asleep.

When I emerged from my hibernation my face had swelled, adding a mixture of The Elephant Man and Quasimodo to my look. A strange sense of clarity overtook me as I looked at myself in the bathroom mirror. All the decisions I had made to this point were either terrible or shortsighted. I wasn't cut out for whatever slice of the criminal pie I had carved for myself here in Harbor Point. Yeah, I could throw my hands better than most but where had that gotten me? Half dead with nothing to show for it. I was done with it all. The gangsters, pimps and ladies of the night could stay far away from me and let me get on with whatever my life was to become. I dumped the remainder of the painkillers into the toilet and flushed. I flicked the light off and left the room, actually believing that line of bullshit.

.   .   .

Desperately I tried, and failed most of the time, to not think about Cherry and what had happened on the boat. There were too many unanswerable questions and the more I thought about it the more I wished I hadn't flushed those painkillers. What was this good cause they yammered on about and how did Cherry and Buckshot get tangled up in whatever that was? As long as I had known Cherry there was always a bigger fish at the end of the line. Maybe that's what this was. It was the only logical explanation that my mind could come up with as to why those two would get involved with someone like Cathy Meyer. It wouldn't surprise me if in the near future there was a newscast or an article in the local paper that reported Ms. Meyer joining her husband in the great beyond. Of course there'd be no mention of the money or her two accomplices and Buckshot and Cherry would be perfectly fine with that.

Keeping in line with my new resolution to play it as straight as possible I resigned myself to let them go and act like they didn't exist. My constitution for taking shots to the head or dodging bullets was not what it used to be and so the idea of chasing these nuts all over the map was not something I had any interest in.

It was not as easy to just walk away from everything that happened. Takeoff and Evelyn, at my behest, had come to my apartment. When I opened the door there was little need for explanation but I gave it to them anyway. I had scraped together whatever money I had laying around, mostly earned from my employment with the Kreski's, and gave them about five grand each. Both protested but there was no way that cash was coming back my way. Evelyn was not happy about having to return to the pole at The Cheetah but she was grateful for the money and stayed to cook me dinner that night. She was good people and someone I could rely on no matter what. Takeoff seemed a little out of sorts with what happened at the warehouse. He took his money, shook my hand and left. Last I heard he hadn't shown up for any of his gigs at the club and no one had seen or heard from him.

I handled Wheels myself. Armed with an arsenal of cleaning supplies I hit the warehouse and when I was finished no one would be the wiser. In the end Wheels found a resting place in the marshes and the van had mysteriously caught fire in an abandoned lot in The Bottoms.

I was in the kitchen feeding Boris when I saw Mr. Ortiz ascending the steps to my landing. He struggled with a large box and a plastic bag in his arms. The door was open slightly and he nudged it with his knee, letting himself in. Oddly, after all that had happened, we had become closer. Not simply neighbors who shot around small talk but actual friends who shared things mere acquaintances wouldn't.

He set the box on the floor, ran a hand along Boris' eager head and laid the bag on the table. The smell was the truest form of food intoxication. The silverware had already been laid out for our weekly dining ritual. I grabbed a couple of cold beers from the fridge and joined Mr. Ortiz, who was already seated and smiling.

"Is a joyous day my friend but some melancholy I feel at your table," he said in his cryptically broken English.

"Like good news or bad news," I said, taking a seat and digging into a container of the best chili relleno in the world.

"Maybe...maybe," he said, filling his plate and mouth before continuing, "but is not all bad. My daughter is getting married."

The smile was so wide on his face that little chunks of food had nowhere to go but from his mouth and onto his shirt. I had been hearing about these impending nuptials for a few weeks but for reasons not known to either of us this boy his daughter was seeing had not popped the question.

We raised our glasses and celebrated his family amongst Boris's protestations from below the table. Mexican was not good for his little stomach. The bad news, as I would soon find out, was that Mr. Ortiz and the entire Ortiz clan was leaving Harbor Point and going south to be closer to his daughter. I was happy for them and would miss my friend but was secretly happy that they were leaving this place.

It was late when he left and we were both drunk. We exchanged a long hug and I expressed a willingness to help them pack up in anyway I could. I shut the door behind him and would have forgotten all about the box save for the fact that I smashed my foot against it and fell to the floor.

I slid it close to inspect it. There was no return address and the thought that it might be a bomb or some dangerous chemical never occurred to me as I ripped at the packing tape that held the top flaps closed. It could be described as a big box and once I got the top open a fair amount of shredded newspaper came with it. I peered inside and held my breath.

A shrink wrapped block of one hundred dollar bills sat at the bottom on a nest of more shredded newspaper. I didn't breathe for a long time, my eyes transfixed on a yellow sticky note on top of the cash. The scrawl was in neat red ink and read:

I'll explain it all one day.

Cherry

My stomach churned at the sight of her name. I fought off the impulse to think about where she was when she sent the package and what prompted it? I couldn't do it. I grabbed the note, crumpled it in my fist and tossed it across the room. There had to be two hundred, two hundred and fifty thousand in that pack, at least. Not enough to get me to my island doing nothing for the rest of my life but better than where I was five minutes ago. Maybe this money could help me walk the straight line for good this time? I thought about all the things I could do with the money when Boris hopped over my shoulder directly into the box. He twisted back and forth, got comfortable and sat down on the money. His purr was deafening as he shot me an apathetic look. I couldn't help but laugh to myself.

He always did like her better.

I would like to sincerely thank you for reading *Cold Hard Cash*. To show my gratitude, I would like to give you a copy of **Rabbit Punch** for free (eBook only unfortunately). The book is an exclusive and only offered to readers of *Cold Hard Cash* —that's you!

Rabbit Punch is a prequel and tells the story of the end of Ellis's boxing career and how he came to Harbor Point. You'll also find out how Boris the cat came into Ellis's life.

You can get it here: **daledevino.com/rabbitpunch**

GET EXCLUSIVE ACCESS

Sign up for my reader mailing list for your free copy of
Stick Em' Up **(Ellis Boone #0).**
You'll get early access and news pertaining to the Harbor Point
Crime Series. This includes Advanced Reader Copies, artwork
and discounts.

Many of these deals & offers will only be available through my
newsletter.
Sign up at **daledevino.com**

My goal is to get to know my readers, not just try to sell you
books. No spam. EVER.

The citizens of Harbor Point are its lifeblood. They make it unique, interesting, and a little dangerous. Like me, you have now prowled the streets and gotten a taste for the place. I hope you'll visit again. It's a big city with lots of avenues and dark alleys to explore.

As a reader you are in a position to help Harbor Point and ensure that it thrives and continues to grow. Reviews and word of mouth are the currency that authors and indie publishers like myself survive on. If no one reads the books should I continue to write them? That's up to the readers and fans.

So, if you enjoyed *Cold Hard Cash* I would ask you to consider leaving a review and lend a hand to the people of The Point. It's a rough city and they could use your support.

Thank you for reading *Cold Hard Cash* and maybe we'll run into each other on the boardwalk.

Cold Hard Cash almost didn't get written. I initially wrote half of it and could not tell if it was any good or worthy of eyeballs other than my own. I sent what I had to a trusted friend and he gave it a read. When he implored me to finish it because he needed to know how it ended I knew I might be onto something. I wasn't exactly sure what it would turn into but I knew I just had to complete it. As I neared the end I got an idea for a second book and then a third and the series was born.

I think the reason I like writing about this place is that I genuinely like Ellis Boone. He's not a good guy but he's definitely not a villain either. He's just a guy in the world trying to survive the best way he knows how. Does he always make the smart and sensible choice? No, but how many of us do that with any consistency?

So I hope you enjoyed this first foray into the world of Harbor Point and didn't end up in the Kreski's basement. There are many more stories to come with characters you've met or will meet in the future.

I have to get back to writing. Ellis is ready to tell me what he's going to do next.

ACKNOWLEDGMENTS

There are a few key individuals that need their names somewhere in this book. The concept of Ellis Boone and Harbor Point came from my brain but it doesn't make it to the page without these people.

Clarke Mayer - You know what you mean to this project. You provided unwavering support, encouragement, and endless availability to talk shop for countless hours. This book doesn't exist without you. You're the perfect creative partner and a great friend.

George Spetz - your time, opinions, and ideas were a key part of making *Cold Hard Cash* a reality. You read this thing before I even knew what it was and didn't hang up on me when I babbled on and on endlessly. If it sucked I knew you'd tell me to my face and that means more than anything.

Kimberly Kocher - Without your eagle eyes and attention to detail I sincerely don't know if I would have made it over the last hill to publication. Someone who is willing to edit your work relentlessly and motivate at the same time is invaluable. You're both of those things and I thank you for that.

Ellis Boone returns in *Pennies From Heaven*.

www.ingramcontent.com/pod-product-compliance
Lightning Source LLC
Chambersburg PA
CBHW050348190726

48284CB00007BB/2195